I0629977

TABOO V

YONDER

Published by
THE HARRISON GROUP

TABOO 5. Copyright 2014 by Yonder. All rights reserved.

THE CHRONICLES OF YOUNG LANCE. Copyright 2014 by T.L. Rawlings.

This book is a work of fiction. Names, characters, places, and incidents are the products of the authors' imagination or are used fictitiously. Any resemblance to actual events, locals, or persons living or dead, is entirely coincidental.

All rights reserved. No part of this book may be used or reproduced in any manner whatsoever without written permission except in the case of brief quotations embodied in critical articles and reviews.

Cover design by Nikki Curry for Versitel Photography

Interior design by Jessica Tilles for TWA Solutions

Printed in the United States of America

ISBN 13: 978-0-976772-4-7

For more information, visit us online:
www.yonderpresents.com

ACKNOWLEDGMENTS

First I need to thank God; without him there would be no me.

My "thank yous" are few, with a more realistic approach of who really helped me.

My unconditional lover...

Judy Samantha Harrison. Sometimes you were the blood that flowed through my veins, but God loved you more. May you keep making people smile as you brighten up heaven. My days and spirit are stress-free because of YOU. I celebrate twenty-two awesome years with you and two terrific kids. May the heavens forever shine now that you have arrived.

Rojena and Robert, the other angels watching over me, love you always.

Now the humans: Michelle Coles-Johnson, Jessica Tilles, Troy Rawlings , Kayla Harrison, Rodney Harrison Jr, Austin and Danielle Henderson, Tonya and Tania Frederick, Marvin Wray, Pat Goree, Ruth, Kristin, Marsha ,Maurice, Pete, Ryan, Brandon, Melvin, Robyn, Rocky, Ronda Brian, Christopher, Michael, and Hollywood and Ryze radio family.

The Chronicles of Young Lance

by T.L. Rawlings

College Orientation

We lived for the weekend like adults who worked stressful 9 to 5 workdays for 40 plus hours per week. Well, Robbie and Rob (no relation) were the oldest of our crew and they actually did work 40 hours per week. But Los, Vince and I were the High-Schoolers. Yet when I think about it, we did go to school all day and work 4 hours at night...so yes, we deserved a fucking good time on the weekends, too! And boy did we exploit every possible opportunity to have and define what fun meant to The Bone Daddies. Yes, The Bone Daddies. If I remember correctly, our crew's name came from a Native Tongue Party Ritual of "Grabbing our BONES and start swinging our hands..." – see "Buddy" by De La Soul circa 1989. It's a dick thing...we were young.

Our weekends started on Friday night around 8:00 p.m., with dance rehearsal because you just had to be able to dance in the early '90s...the shit was cool then. And then, the libations; usually

Private Stock, Old E, Brass Monkey, Mickeys, and our favorite Adult-Kool-Aid…Boone's Farm! Y'all don't understand! Boone's Farm goes with any weekend meal. Be it a chicken box with fries, or a 7-11 chili cheese big bite with Doritos, Boone's Farm was the elixir that calmed the savage thirst and gave just the right amount of buzz to make us feel cool as shit.

Now by the time we left to finally head to our first party spot of the weekend it was about 10:00 p.m. and our first stop was UMBC. Yes, lawd! College party!! I loved college parties because I love people, and where else can you get every nationality, culture, and social class in one place partying together? On Friday night, college parties it seemed like everyone just blended in together. It was like when Cyrus was speaking in *The Warriors*… You had the Nerds next to the Jocks, the Round-The-Way girls next to the Studious Freaks, The Q-Dogs next to The Pretty Boys… "Nobody wasting nobody." And best of all, High Schoolers chilling with College kids. The rule of thumb was to stay covert. Just shut up and know how to dance! And that's what The Bone Daddies were all about; we believed in having fun and we could make any dance floor our own.

There were always groups of friends who danced in packs. They even practiced little dance routines together to show off at the party. Then you had the professional dance crews. Street dancers turned hired entertainers at birthday parties and as background dancers for local and national singers and rappers. And umm The Bone Daddies fell somewhere in between. So as you could imagine, the '90s weekend parties were off the chain. Always great stories that carried you through the week until the next Friday! Living for the weekend.

I remember the Friday I met Jasmin. She was in her second year at UMBC, a Biology major, and a Kappa Sweetheart (I would later find out what that meant). I can't say I remember how we locked eyes, started dancing, or how all of our friends left us alone on the gymnasium floor...but it happened pretty much just like that. It was so natural; it was like we'd known each other forever. What's funny is that as I think back I've never had any rap, or a pick-up line of any sort. Just a great fucking personality...ha! It's easy, I make a funny face or catch eyes and say hi... with my hips. Come on y'all know...at a party you walk up, or should I say dance up, to a girl and if she smiles, throws her hips your way, and dances up to you too, IT'S ON!!

"About time!" Jasmin announced smartly.

"About time? What?" I asked, knowing what was coming next.

"You've been looking at me looking at you dancing all night! What does a girl have to do throw something at you?" She chuckled.

"Oh you're saying I'm slow."

"Um yeah…exactly."

We both had to laugh. And by this time we're grinding and jamming to the music. Let me just say that I love the smell of a girl's sweat. The sweet smell of her perfume or scented lotion muddled with the essence of her intense pleasure dripping from her pores…*mmmm yes*. And while dancing close to her, just lowering my nose close to her ear…her neck… her breasts. All of a sudden, the music drowns into heartbeats. Pulse. Us trying to press through our jeans to satisfaction. We're fucking in front of everyone and no one cares because they're doing it, too. So sexy right now. And then Jasmin turned around to put her soft, round ass right up against my throbbing, hard, young manhood. Wooo! Let's Go! DJ Frank Ski is killing on the wheels! Even those folks who never dance were driven to the floor by the rhythm and pounding bass.

"Check This Out... GIRL I'LL HOUSE YOU... GIRL I'LL HOUSE YOU...GIRL I'LL HOUSE YOU...YOU IN MY HUT NOW, MY HUT! WHEN YOU'RE IN MY HUT, YOU KNOW WHAT'S UP...LET YOUR MIND BE FREE... RELAX YOUR BODY..."

As the Jungle Brothers preach through those huge concert speakers, the ladies in the building obeyed. Relaxing their bodies, their curves, their wonderfullness to every command. The music was so hypnotic that it made us feel up every part of our dance partners' bodies. And girls have it so good, no one knows how wet they are under their clothes. Girls be dripping puddles of lust all down their legs, drenching their tight, stone-washed jeans and we'd never know. Unless, of course, you're dancing so close to her that you feel her heartbeat speed up and feel the panting of her breath on your neck.

And when Jasmin turned around; her hips moved like an Egyptian Belly-dancing-Gypsy Woman. Not just enticing me, and commanding my hips to sway with hers, but literally grabbing my hands and putting them on her plump breasts. Her nipples rock hard. And as I squeeze she rears back, her body saying *yes, more...harder*. And I gladly give her more.

11

Now a great DJ not only blends rhythms that seem to be one continuous groove when the party is at its hottest climax, he also has all the essential party tools. Strobe lights, with colors, sirens…and one thing I loved that Frank Ski would bring—a smoke machine with Tropical scented smoke. Boooooooyyyyeeee. Just at the time when you need a sexual healing smoke screen… Poooofff. Bodies turn into unrecognizable silhouettes. Thumping and humping and grooving to the music. Lost in Soul!! How could we not be turned on??

As she rest her back on my chest, I had to ask, "What's your name?"

"Jasmin."

"I'm Lance. Nice to meet you."

We laughed, realizing we had mentally and damn near physically went *waaaay* beyond a first name basis. She turned around and put her arms around my neck. I put my arms around her waist, wrists on her glorious hips, hands resting on her amazing booty…politely though, I'm a gentleman.

"You go here?" she asked.

"No, I'm a youngin. I'm still in high school."

"OH, YOU'RE A BABY?!" jasmine said jokingly. "Oh shoot, I'm gonna get locked up messing with you!"

"No you won't! I won't tell anyone I hooked up with an old woman."

"What?! Old!?"

"Hey you started with the baby stuff!" I said, chuckling.

"Well, you seem mature, and you FEEL grown," Jasmin said, looking me dead in my eyes.

Everyone with blood running through their veins knows this look. It's that look that says, *Come here...kiss me...* And I've never been one to stifle youthful spontaneity. Slow, soft, slightly wet... perfect.

"MMmmm..." Jasmin sighed as we parted lips slowly. "Okay."

As if to say...*yeah... I might give you some.* She was only a few years older than me, but in college and high school years that can seem like decades. But, the more I shut up and let our bodies do the talking and listen to her, the closer our connection became and the less the ages mattered. And I was a 6'1" young man with an athletic build, hanging with 20-somethings, so I seemed to be getting good approval marks in her collegiate mind.

For the rest of the night into the morning, we grooved together between whispered talking in each other's ear. That pertinent information to make sure you're on the same page. We both didn't want to waste time seeing if this attraction was worth it. As the party was ending we went to our separate corners to consult our teams.

"Yeeeaaahhhhh, booooyeee. I seen you hemmed up by the Chocolate hunny all night. Does she go here?" Robbie asked.

"Yes. She's a Bio major, and a Kappa Sweetheart??" I said.

"Oh shit, she's dating a frat dude," Robbie said.

"Word? She didn't say anything about him. As a matter of fact she said she didn't have a boyfriend."

"She might be just boning him." Robbie laughed.

Robbie was the Wise One of the crew. He was the oldest at 24, made the most money and kept the most beautiful women around. He was a pussy magnet and cool as shit. That's hard to find anywhere, a dude that will coach you in the ways of the Jedi and he was a gentleman. The cool thing about my crew also is that we didn't pressure each other into getting with as many chics as possible. We realized if we were having fun and being ourselves, all we had to do is let nature take its course.

"So you gonna fuck her or what?" Rob asked.

"Damn, nigga! Hopefully, I don't know?" I laughed.

Now Rob was pretty much the opposite of Robbie. Robbie is 6 foot; Rob is 5'3". Robbie was a girl magnet…well… you get the point. But they were best friends, go figure.

So the plan was to leave UMBC, grab a bite, and cruise down to North Avenue to catch the sights. Cars, women and winos. Hit Odell's and then Fantasies. But my dick, mind and body wanted to chill with Jasmin…SHIT!

"Yo, Shit…. I'll be back!" I yelled, as I ran back into the lobby. In all the end-of-party excitement I forgot to get Jasmin's number. I saw several fine ass girls while I was dipping through all the social classes and denominations. And then this cute redbone said…

"Hi Lance."

"Hey…Hi…" I said, trying to figure out where I knew her from.

"She's over there…" She pointed to Jasmin who was walking away from a crew of girls all wearing the same sweatshirts.

"I thought you got scared and ran home," Jasmin said, smiling as we gave a good-bye hug.

"Naw I just didn't want to miss my ride, so I..." Before I could finish, she kissed me on the cheek, and slid a piece of paper in my pocket.

"Call me later, baby." She she walked away with her crew.

Now though I wasn't big on bragging about any girl I had been with sexually, maaaaannn....there's something about a College Girl that just...woooo.

Our night continued on, and as the fun continued I felt real good. I couldn't wait to get home to call Jaz. Since she was in college I didn't figure she had a telephone curfew. College girl. While we were at the party, she said she had a roommate who was real cool, so it wouldn't be a problem if I wanted to come by. I was hoping to come by immediately after the party, but those niggas would have left me. Couldn't miss my ride and be stuck out in the boonies on a Friday night. When we were chilling on North Avenue, Rob pulled me aside.

"Yo, I was talking to one of your girl's friends. I may drive back up here Sunday. Find out if she wants you to come," Rob said on the low.

"Cooool, yeah, I'll find out when I call her."

Rob didn't want everyone to know we were coming back, who knows why. It wasn't like Robbie and Los didn't have shit to do. But it might have been because he didn't want us to step to his girl... or she wasn't that cute. Who knows?? I just know I was gonna see Jasmin again.

We talked almost all day Saturday. Fresh and fun conversation and several "You're pretty mature for your age..." from her. Having a brother 10 Years older and friends who were 21 plus helped me think and talk older than the average 16 year old. I just felt like I belonged. And during the conversation I realized Jasmin, although older, was all girl. And she was excited to see me, too.

Sunday couldn't come soon enough and Rob came and got me early Sunday afternoon. Rob's parents were well off and he still lived at home. There were all kinds of perks he got since he was finishing culinary school, like his new candy apple red Jetta. If the girls didn't like Rob's looks or demeanor, usually having his own cool-ass ride helped his rap. He pulled up, music blasting and all the windows down. It was a warm, fall day and beautiful outside. And Rob had just washed and waxed the Jetta. Rob was cool sometimes, but lord, when this nigga started bragging you'd want to shoot him... NIGGA SHUT UP!! Other than that he was cool.

"Yo, so your girl Jasmin's friend's name is Angie. Did you see me dancing with her?" Rob asked.

"Umm, I can't remember. How did she look?"

"Tall chick, long legs, long hair…brown skin…"

"Yes, I did see her after the party; she was over hanging with Jasmin. They all had those sweatshirts on. She was a cutie! Awww shucks!"

"What?" Rob asked.

"What? What?" I asked back.

"Why do you sound surprised?" Rob asked.

"What…I'm not, I'm just saying she was fine and tall," I said trying to get out of…

"Yo, my arm is strong, son. Y'all be sleeping on me, son," Rob continued.

"I'm woke…" I mumbled.

"Huh?" Rob asked.

"I said I hear that."

We jammed to the radio and got to UMBC campus pretty quick. I realized everything is closer during the day when you can see where you're going. It actually wasn't that far at all. The girl who Rob was going to see was Angie and she told him they would be at the celebrity basketball game. When we got to the game, Jasmin, Angie and some other ladies were actually working one of the fundraising booths. Rob and I had synchronized our pagers and watches, that meant no matter what let's meet back down at the cafe area at 9:00 p.m.! When the ladies spotted us, Jasmin came right over to me as I was walking to her.

"Hi, Rob!" Jasmin said, as she grabbed my hand and escorted me back out the door.

All I could do was laugh. "What in the world?? Why did you pull me out of there?" I asked.

"I am not trying to spend another 2 hours at that booth. You actually saved me, baby," Jasmin said right before she stopped so we could give each other a hug and a sweet peck on the lips. I say sweet because I could feel her heartbeat.

"Alright, so I'm going to give you the quickie tour."

Jasmin escorted me through her version of the official school tour. Pretty much the places she had class and frequented and pointed out the different Clubs' hangout areas around campus. She was gorgeous. I mean, I'm a little different than most guys I think because it's not just outer beauty that gets me. I love chemistry, and connection. And Jaz made my nature rise, literally.

"And finally, this is my dorm; my home away from home. It's Co-ed, which is cool. We don't have the security drama of all-girl dorms."

"You mean you can run dudes in and out…"

"Exactly!" Jaz said, as we laughed.

Since I wasn't a student they just made me sign in and leave my ID at the front desk. As soon as we got in her room, I pulled Jasmin close to me and gave her a real kiss. Our tongues made love in our mouths. Jasmin moaned as if we were already having sex, which turned me on so much I moaned back! What the fuck? I don't know if I had ever really made a sexual sound while kissing before. I was always so busy listening for the girl's erotic noises and body quakes.

"Wait…wait…" she panted.

"Yes," I answered still kissing her neck.

"My roommate is coming back."

Okay, I've always had a thing for having sex with other people in the room. That never bothered me, actually, just the opposite. I loved it.

Jasmin pulled away and asked, "Okay…woo… what kind of music do you like? I mean do you like Old School?"

"Of course I do!" I answered, excited with a rock hard dick.

Jasmin popped in a slow jam tape. The first joint was easy, Guy's "Piece of My Love."

"I hope you're not trying to challenge my knowledge of old school music because you might just lose," I said to her, confident in my skills.

"Oh really, we'll see," she answered.

"OH SNAP!! IS THAT YOU?" I asked as a picture on a photo-album cover had caught my eye.

For the next hour we listened to slow jams, and laughed at her old high school photos and yearbooks. In between we would take 5 and 10 minute make-out breaks...until the books were on the floor with our shoes, and we were kissing, sucking, licking and fondling nonstop.

"Do you have a condom?" she asked.

"Yes," I said.

Thank you Jesus, I thought. I never ever think I'm going to actually have sex. No...really! It keeps me from getting upset if a girl says stop; even if we're actually fucking, NO MEANS NO! Thanks, Mom, for sticking that in my head.

It was getting dark and the only light was coming from her stereo and her digital clock. I was indulged in sucking on Jaz's big beautiful titties while dipping my finger into her moist, juicy pussy. As her pants changed to moans of ecstasy, her pussy went from moist to wet to creamy as her body began to contort and jerk like she was possessed. Oh my God, I was loving pleasing her, but her hand had my rock hard dick in a death grip with no lubrication. OUCH…but I couldn't stop, I was too turned on by her cumming down my arm, on the bed…and then, the door opened slowly…

Jasmin jumped up and covered herself with the covers. All I could do was laugh as her roommate walked in… it was the redbone from the party.

"I'm sorry, y'all. I have to grab my Psych book. Sorry," Tara said, acting embarrassed.

"Tara…girl…oh my God…girl…" Jasmin could hardly get her words straight.

"Hi, Lance, I'm sorry, and umm…" Tara looked down at my dick.

Damn. In all the commotion Mr. Man was just watching everything as if to say, *Is it my turn yet, finger's getting all the goodness.*" I just laughed and grabbed some covers. We all kind of laughed and then…there was a knock at the door. A code type of knock.

Knock knock…knock knock knock knock and then a male's voice.

"Hey, Jaz," he whispered.

By how big the girls' eyes got as they looked at each other, I quickly thought this must be the Kappa looking for his sweetheart. Before I could react the two girls went into action. Jasmin kissed me and jumped in the bathroom and Tara took her shirt and pants off and pulled me on her bed.

Then she whispered, "Take your shit off."

Yes, ma'am!" I quickly did as I was told until I was in Tara's bed butt assed naked!!

Tara poked her head out the door and said, "Todd, your timing sucks…"

"What the fuck are you talking about, Tara? Jimmy told me he saw Jaz come up here about 2 hours ago. If she doesn't want to talk, fuck it."

Before Todd could finish Tara pulled the door open wide and said, "You want to meet my guest?!" Tara said, with attitude.

As the dude peeked around the door to Tara's bed, I was acting like I was asleep, naked as all life. Then I turned like I was getting up. Todd backed out the door in a hurry.

"Girl you a freak! I didn't need to see that!" Todd said embarrassed.

"Tried to tell you," Tara said, laughing. "Check Angie's room!"

As Tara closed the door we were crying laughing. And Tara's body was amazing!!! But I was busy laughing, heart pounding with fear of getting jumped by some frat dudes.

Jaz came out the bathroom and apologized. "I'll be back, y'all," Jasmin said, too embarrassed to look at me. She peeked out the dorm room door and went after Todd.

"Wow. That's crazy…" I said, still shocked.

"Well…no need to let this good dick suffer," Tara said, as she pushed me on her bed and grabbed my dick. She licked the head until my dick woke back up. Then Tara licked and sucked the sides like it was an Astro-pop. I couldn't hold it… I screamed.

"OH MY GOOOOODDD"

I really love college!!!

Taboo 5

––––⋅◦⋅◦⋅––––

A Bowl of Fruit

Recap: When I last talked to you, I was at work, in the bathroom getting my Johnson sucked by a white coworker, Crystal, when someone entered the bathroom....

Even though I was scared, I was coming. Crystal never heard the door open. She was just inhaling, as cum trickled down her face. She was swallowing and I was trying to pull up my pants. That was scary and exciting at the same time. It was exciting because it was dangerous— which made it totally Taboo—and just the thought of getting caught made my dick extra hard. You would think I had a piece of steel in my pants. Now it was also scary because I was at work. What if the person that entered was the big boss, or even worse, one of the other men that work on my floor? He could tell my boss and I could lose my job. Or even worse, he could blackmail me. So, as I return to my senses, I started thinking of a way out of that horny ass mess. How was I going to get out of that bathroom and get Crystal out of here without anyone seeing us? So, that was what I did. I put my hand over her mouth, came out of the stall, and looked around. Whoever it was who came in, had to go really bad. I heard him in the stall, blowing out and grunting. I grabbed Crystal's hand and we ran out the bathroom together and down the back stairs. We were laughing as we ran down the stairs. We finally arrived to the last set of steps. I told Crystal we couldn't do that anymore. We both laughed and walked to her car.

Pause: I think I need to put the brakes on that relationship with Crystal....

BTS:
Then Devin kicked in, saying, "Henny, we gonna keep that girl forever. Do you know the benefits of having a white girl that adores you?"

I said, "No Devin. Explain."

"Remember how you got this job?"

"Yes. I knew someone."

"Right. Remember, there are not a whole lot of men in this building. So knowing someone like

Crystal will eventually have its advantages…in getting a promotion and maybe your next job."

Pause: I thought about what Devin said. He really had some solid points.

BTS:
So, now I decided not to end it with Crystal. So since I was still sitting in her car, we started at it in the parking lot. Mind you, it was nine o'clock in the morning. We started touching and feeling each other like we were teenagers. We were so hot and heavy, the windows had fogged up. The energy in her car was incredible. She pulled my slacks down and she was back at it.

Pause: I always thought it was a rumor or urban myth. But white girls like sucking dick more than anything.

BTS:
So that time, I wanted some pussy instead. I pulled her skirt up and touched her pussy. Then I looked at it and realize it was pretty. It was not just pretty. It was beautiful. I had never seen a clean-shaven pussy before. I immediately started coming.

"What's going on, Henson?" she asked, with my dick in her hand, as I was flooding her hands like I was peeing. I can't even speak.

So, of course, Devin kicked and said, "Lick that dick — lick it now!"

She did just as she was instructed. I loved every minute of it. I had the pussy closer to me so I started to touch it. I didn't really know what to do with eating pussy because I had never eaten anyone.

Pause: I have seen it done in movies and in my father's Playboy *magazines. But, I have never done it myself.*

BTS:
So I started to go down on her. I licked and licked. Then I heard a loud commotion, sounding like a big boom.

"Get out of the car," he said, as if on a loud speaker or bullhorn. "Please exit the car. Please exit the car now!"

The End

Trying to live right
Trying to be good
But why
Excitement and the big "O"
Are what I live 4

I am going through something
I have gotten over something
I am getting better
Have been faithful
I want to be good

Life has given me too many choices
I wonder is this just a Maggie issue
Or is what everybody do

Taboo

Maggie's Madness

The Metamorphosis of a Whore

Recap: When I last talked to you, I was in the motel room with Freight Train and Quida. Quida was in the process of completing her assignment and I was assisting. The assignment was similar to the one I did for Professor Kindred. (Topic: What really turns a man on?) Her assignment: Make a man lose control.

BTS:
I was in my car outside the motel. I left Quida in the room. I could not take it anymore. After all the condoms broke with me trying to do Freight Train, I decided to leave.

Fate Or Luck

Trying to do all the wrong things
For all the wrong reasons
Condoms broke
No more action for me

Should I be happy
Sad — disappointed
Or just mad
Some say if it was not for bad luck
They wouldn't have any luck
But me, Maggie
It has to be fate
Because I am growing a conscience
If that's possible
I don't want to live this way
So I ask
Is it luck or fate
That my life is this way

BTS:

I arrive home with guilt written all over my face.
And of course, everyone was home. I started
to realize that I liked being a mother and wife
more than anything. I didn't want to be a whore

anymore. My daughters, Renee and Rojena, met me at the door.

"Mommy, we are so glad you are home. Daddy has a surprise for all of us," they said.

I was anxious and a little nervous. Hell, as trifling as I had been, I didn't deserve a husband or children that loved me so much. I followed them into the living room.

My husband yelled, "We are going on a family vacation to Disney World!"

I blurted, "Disney World?!"

He said, "Yes, was that okay?"

I broke down crying uncontrollably. How

could someone love me that much? Now I was on my knees, sobbing and weeping.

My children were holding me, asking, "What's wrong, Mommy?"

My husband held my hand. "Baby, was everything okay? I can change the location to the Bahamas or some other place."

I couldn't stop crying.

Crying
It's flowing like water
I can't stop it
It will not stop
Tears constantly flowing
Thoughts, visions, just feelings
Of being inadequate
Thoughts of just not
Deserving to be loved
So here I sit on the floor
Still crying

BTS:
Once I got myself together and could actually talk, my husband and children were still holding me. I told them how much I loved and cared for them, and that I wanted them to be proud of me.

Renee said, "Mommy, we are always proud of you and we love you."

"Maggie, I am so proud to have you as my wife and you are an excellent role model for our girls. I appreciate you raising them most of the time by yourself because I work so much." His words picked up my spirits. Even though I felt so guilty, I started to feel just a little better.

Unconditional Love

What is it
Is it something
That folks just
Dream about
Can someone actually
Love you
Even though you are
A true piece of work
And didn't seem like
You are getting better
I thought God
Only provide that
Can a human have
The same love
As God has for us

BTS:
Once I finally stopped crying, we all hugged. I told
the girls how much I loved them and my husband
told me he had something special for us tonight.
He had a babysitter for the children and dinner
plans for us on the Spirit of Washington.

Pause: Spirit of Washington is a cruise ship that cruises

through the waters of Washington, DC and Northern Virginia, bypassing all the major monuments. Lunch and dinner are served with dancing – a Motown Review.

BTS:

I was excited. So we packed the girls up and took them next door to our neighbors—Julisa and Frederick Santos. They were from the Virgin Islands and had children the same ages as ours.

Flashback:

A few years ago, when both of our mates were out of town, Frederick made a pass at me. Initially, I did not respond. But, the next time I saw him, he said, "Maggie, I apologize for making a pass at you. I respect you and your marriage. Can I be honest with you?"

"Please do. But can I call you "FF"?"

"What does that stand for?"

"Freaky Freddy."

We both laughed.

Then I told him to be honest and tell me what was on his mind.

"Here it is. Maggie, I would like to make love to your pussy."

"Explain that."

He said his wife does not like to be eaten. So he would like to make love via his mouth to my pussy at least once a month. I was stunned but, I appreciated his honesty.

"Only under certain conditions will I consider your request."

"Okay, what are they? I will agree to almost anything."

"You have to make me come each time."

"I can do that…"

"You have to pay me $200 each time."

"I've got that," he said smugly.

"I have to pick the date, time and place."

He nodded.

"When I say I no longer want your services, you must leave and act like it never happened. Cool?"

"Cool."

Freaky Freddy agreed to all the terms. So, we started meeting once a month for him to eat 'til his heart was content, and for me to collect my money, which I usually gave to the girls — $100 a piece — because I always felt good, but also guilty.

BTS:

We talk to the Santos' for a little while longer while "FF" was just smiling ear to ear.

Pause: I let FF lick me in the storage shed in my backyard last week. And damn, he can eat some coochie! But I had to put an end to it. That was his last time.

BTS:
We got the girls situated. I thanked the Santos'. We kissed the girls goodbye and we were on our way back over to the house. My thoughts were to break him off real good before we got on the boat ride. So I put both of our outfits on the bed while he got in the shower. While he was in the shower, I stepped in there, washed off all my goodies, and told him I wanted to do something special for him. He was all smiles. I was also. I retrieved the Boatmen's throat lozenges from the cabinet under the sink in the cabinet—singers and people that do public speaking use Boatmen's, as one lozenge is so strong, it will open up all the pores and when you inhale, you feel it all the way to your toes. I put three in my mouth and told him to get out of the shower. I told him to go sit on the bed, naked and wet. He does as instructed. I sucked on the throat lozenges for about two more minutes, spit out two,

and left one in my mouth. I left the bathroom. He was on the bed waiting. I told him to lie sideways across the bed. I crawled up the bed like a snake. I started licking the side of his leg and ass. Once I got up close to his dick, instead of sucking right away, I licked into the crevices that hold the dick. The crevices are like little pockets.

Pause: Let me explain deeper — on each side of the dick, there are little openings. On a woman, it's the same.

BTS:
So as I licked the pockets, his dick stood to attention. I cupped his big balls in my hand and gave them a sucking worthy of an Olympic gold medal. He loved that so much; I saw tears streaming down his face. As he cried, I stopped and cried with him.

"Why did you stop, Maggie? It was feeling so damn good."

"I didn't know, babe. It was like you were in pain and I felt it."

"No, Maggie, there is no pain. These are tears of joy, but also tears of guilt. Joy because you have made me so happy since the first day I met you and all through my life." Before I could ask what he was guilty of, he completed his thought. "I am guilty of never spending enough time with you and the girls. I feel like I have been cheating and the business was the other woman, constantly keeping me out late and making me leave home early."

Now I was crying like a baby. How was it that that man, my husband had finally heard my prayers?

Pause: I needed to pray. "Dear God, it was Maggie. I know I always come when I need something, but this time I am coming here to thank You. Thank You for saving a wretch like me. Amen, Amen, Amen!"

BTS:

I needed to start going back to church. God had always taken care of me and I couldn't get my sorry ass up on Sundays to go to church. I was planning to go that Sunday. I looked at the clock and realized we needed to leave soon. So we both started to get dressed. I let him know that I would finish him off later tonight. We were finally dressed — him, with a cream-colored, linen two piece pant set. I had on a cream and brown sundress to match his outfit. It had spaghetti straps and my pumps were fierce. They complimented the dress. Hell, they took over the outfit! They were so bad, my husband said, "Maggie, you are wearing that dress!" Then he looked down and said, "Damn! Those are some true "fuck-me-pumps"! You have to wear them to bed tonight!"

Pause: Women and Men — always listen to your mate, even when they didn't realize it. He said he wanted to fuck me with the pumps on. He would get his chance real soon. When you listen to your mate, they will tell you all the things you would need to know to turn them out totally. And trust me; everyone wants to be totally turned out!

BTS:
So I suggested instead of driving to the waterfront, that we catch a taxicab.

He asked, "Why, when we have luxury cars? I bought you that Mercedes for events like that—so we can show off."

I put my hand over his lips and whispered in his ear. "You can have some ass tonight."

He dropped the keys immediately! Now we were on our way out of the front door. We walked to the nearest cross street, which was 18th Street.

Within two minutes, we were in a taxicab and on our way. We gave the driver the location. We were relaxing and then my husband started to get frisky. I really wanted to give him head right there in the taxicab. But, I was trying to be "good" Maggie.

Pause: I had other stuff planned for him on that boat ride that would surely blow his mind.

BTS:
So, I slowed him down and whispered, "If you can't wait for a few hours for what I have planned for you, I will make you get me an upgraded Mercedes. I am tired of driving that 190E series."

"Well, Maggie, you have to be willing to do something spectacular to get a Mercedes upgrade!"

Now he was talking trash and I loved it! So, I fed into it.

"Remember how good that pussy really is."

He responds, "How good do you really think it is?"

"As far as I know, it's the sweetest in the world. That's why I call it "Sweetness" — because there was nothing sweeter!"

Now the cab driver was laughing. I almost forgot we were still in the cab. So, since Maggie was always so bold, I got the cab driver involved and asked him what made him laugh.

He responded, "I have never heard a woman be that bold about her skills." He then said, "I have dropped off hookers and strippers and they are not that bold either. I heard you say your name was Maggie. Maggie, you are mad!"

I laughed. My husband liked when I was a tease and he encouraged it. So I asked, "Why would you call me made? Is that mad, as in madness?

He responded, "Yes, to talk about your sexuality openly. I would say it was madness because most women are never that bold."

"They are not Maggie!" I told him.

My husband whispered in my ear. "Leave him alone and give me some head."

I burst out laughing.

Pause: The key to life was to know who you are because eighty-five percent of you are searching, which was why knowing yourself was so important.

BTS:
We were now in front of the Spirit of Washington. My husband paid the driver and then I tipped him by pulling up the back of my dress and gave him

a full view of my *ass*ets — I didn't have on panties! As I turned on my heels and walked to the boat, the cab driver was running up behind me.

"Ms. Madness! Ms. Madness!"

I turned around. "Yes, sir, did we leave something in the cab?"

He grabbed my hand and stuffed a wad of money in it, and ran back to his cab. As the cab pulled off, he blew the horn at me.

"Thank you! Thank you!" he shouted out the window at me.

I caught up with my husband and we proceeded to board the boat.

My husband asked, "What was that about?"

"The cabbie just felt like he owed me a tip."

We both laughed, as we walked up the plank. We took a couple's picture. Damn! We looked good together.

Pause: I need to keep that man forever. Not only was he good in bed and an excellent provider. He was fine on top of all that.

BTS:

We were seated by a young lady and the boat was quickly filling up. We had good seats, so were able to see all the festivities. We dined on a nice five-course meal with drinks, but my husband made a trip to the bar.

Pause: I just realized I never told you my husband's name. His name was Raymond Tally.

BTS:
Raymond returned with two Long Island Iced Teas.

Pause: Drinks with five different liquors bring out all of my horniness and sometimes my whore-ism!

BTS:
As I sipped my drink, my body parts got to moving. My toes were even whistling! *Who knows what may go on with me tonight?* I thought to myself. *I might surprise myself.* Raymond started talking dirty, saying stuff like "Maggie, can we do something kinky when we get to the cab?"

Pause: I told you that women were so much smarter than men. He suggested it. I had already planned out the whole scenario before his suggestion. Maggie was so on top of her game!

BTS:

So there we were on the boat and walking around outside, touching and kissing each other so passionately.

Pause: Fellas, learn how to kiss! This form of intimacy is the beginning to some terrific fucking. Kissing is like the first door to the pussy!

BTS:

So as we kiss deeper, stronger, more intensely, my sweetness was so moist, it was about to leak down my leg. All of my freaky motions and visions started to surface. Damn! I was horny! I had to do something now! Since I had already scoped out everything on the boat, I knew the right place that I would have my latest adventure.

Pause: Maggie always has a plan!!!

BTS:

I planned to turn out Raymond so badly that he would be babbling like a baby. Also with the plan, I wanted to show my exhibition skills. Yes I loved to be watched! I was going to put on a show. I was better than any porn movie you had ever seen!

I r.eturned my focus to Raymond. We went upstairs, and I stroked every part of him and he was trying to put his hand up my dress. So I pushed his hands up to my B-cup breasts. He loved it. So I pulled out my nipple and he lost his mind. So here was my grand finale. I backed into a corner and pulled him closer, got on my knees, licked his dick three times to make sure it was ready for a challenge. Then I switched places with him, got snugly in the corner and dropped my dress completely. He totally flipped out, as he watched it fall down around my feet.

"What...what are you doing, MagMag?!"

I grabbed his dick and pull him closer. His eyes were the size of fifty-cent pieces. I pulled his dick hard, bent over and forced it in my ass. Damn! The head of his dick was so huge. So I had to readjust myself. Now it was in. I started one of my perfect moves.

Pause: Picture this: I raised my ass up just enough to be pointed in his direction. I was on my tiptoes. Once he entered, I was totally flat foot so I could fuck him, too.

BTS:

So as I was doing my moves, he was just frozen... like at dinner. He was mesmerized and loving every minute of it. Instead of him drilling me, I was doing counter-clockwise swirls that were blowing his mind. I looked back at him. His eyes were closed so tight, it looked like he was dead.

"Raymond? Raymond?! You okay?"

He opened his eyes. It was like I had him in a trance. I loved that as much as him.

Pause: Women and men, learn the true skills to turn your mate out.

BTS:

So as I proceeded to give him more than he could handle, I really started feeling myself because I was about to cum and the buildup was so intense.

Pause: Women, having an orgasm while being fucked in the ass was just as powerful as a multi-orgasm. The intensity can cripple you!

BTS:

So since I was feeling myself, I started to move even faster and then I touched my lil girl in the boat and stroke my sweetness extremely fast. Damn! It felt so good. I was about to….

"Umm umm umm…"

…*cooooooooome!*

"Ohhhhhhh! Goddamn! Fuck me, Raymond! Fuck me harder. Harder Yes!!!! Motherfucker, tear that ass up now! Keep fucking! Damn! This feels good."

Raymond was silent at first. Then, he started coaching me.

"Yeah, bend that back. Come and get that dick! Come get more of it!"

He was pounding me. Then he totally flipped on me. I was a little scared, but I was enjoying it. Then, he stopped coaching anymore. Suddenly, he became straight gangster-fucking.

"Bitch, you love that dick, didn't you? This was my ass and my pussy and you bet-not ever share it again!"

He was smacking my ass harder and harder and harder. I was scared, but yet I was enjoying it.

Pause: Wait a minute. Stop the damn presses! Did he say, "Share it again?" Oh, hell, did he know that I had been a true tramp since the day we married? Did he know I was a slut before he married me? Wait a minute, was his ass fucking someone else as well? That would explain why he was always so damn tired and never home. Work my ass; he was fucking someone else...could he have a slew of hos? My mind was going buck wild now!

BTS:

Raymond was talking more shit and getting rougher. I am definitely a freak because I loved it. Instead of him stroking like Long John Silver, he had his whole dick in me and it felt like it was poking at my navel. He was no longer pumping. He was doing a counter-clockwise swirl. He was blowing my mind. I was trying to think about what he said about sharing, but damn, that as some good fucking. Then I tried to hold back, but I couldn't any longer.

"Ahh, ahh, ahhhhhh YESSSS!" I was coming. It felt like I was peeing...shitting...having a stroke... delivering a baby...just pure magic all at the same time. Juices were coming out my ass...out my pussy...slobber coming from my mouth... tears were streaming down my face.

Raymond started to pound even more... even harder. For some reason, I thought he was punishing me. And, yes, I should have been punished. I had been whorish for years. He was handling his business so good, as he was still hitting it, my sweetness was making a smacking sound and he loved the sound. I could tell because he stopped talking to me. He was talking to my ass. Then he pulled me up slightly and put that big dick in the pussy. I could handle this. Sweetness just spilled out and started squirting cum everywhere. That one session of fucking was better than ten men together. He was really handling his business. I just loved that man.

I started to sing "You belong to me. Don't share this that with anyone — anymore. All your head-jobs will be from me. Don't want you touching another pussy or ass. You belong to me."

He surprised me and started talking. "Never ever will you let another see my sweetness, touch another man, or even give him head. You will finish college with honors and start going to church as a family because you belong to me."

I was actually crying now because I thought he knew about the other men and I thought he knew about the two experiments. But he still loved me and was going to stay. He was still fucking me. Would he ever stop? Then out of nowhere, we heard a thunderous applause — twelve people were clapping. We turned around and most of them were half naked or completely naked. I was not sure what was going on. So I put my dress back on.

Pause: Was that some type of nudist boat ride and no one informed us?

BTS:
That nudist boat ride was just my crazy imagination. After I put on my dress, I really wanted to leave, but the boat was still in the middle of the Potomac. But I was really not worried because that was my husband and not one of my experiments. It didn't matter who saw me or who saw me pleasing the only man that truly loved me.

I started asking questions. "What the hell y'all clapping for? Why are you watching us and was that some pornographic movie or something?" Everyone started laughing.

A young woman pulled me to the side and the dude with her, whom I guessed was her husband, pulled Raymond to the side and explained they were a part of a swingers' group called JI (Just Imagine). I was dumbfounded. If my tongue could touch the floor it would have been there.

Pause: A swinger was a group of folks — some married,

and most times with children — who decided that their relationship was strong enough for them to have sex with others, and their spouse can do the same. Afterwards, they all return to their normal lives.

BTS:

Being a swinger sounded good. But I didn't think it was for everyone. I was not knocking them, but personally, I couldn't stand the thought of someone else having my man. Hell, I didn't want someone fucking my man and didn't know them.

As both of us were back in each other's arms, the boat was cruising so fast; we were now at the dock. Once we get off the boat, we were silent. There were taxi cabs waiting at the dock. We hopped in the first cab we saw. I gave the cab driver our address. Our eye contact was kind of disturbing, as if we were trying to reach the other's soul or piercing or even cleansing. I was wondering what he knew about my hoing? But also, who he had been with? Was I still number one? Did he like someone else's pussy better than mine? Now I was no good. But then, I caught myself. Hell no! There was no pussy better than sweetness. You had better ask somebody!

Finally, I broke the silence between us. "Raymond, are you okay?"

"Yes, I am good. How are you MagMag?" Then he asked me if there was anything I needed to tell him. I didn't know if I should answer that question because if I told him the truth, he would be gone and would take the girls with him.

"No," I said, posing him the same question.

"Yes, MagMag, there was something I want to tell you."

Pause: My heart jumped into my feet. What if he told me he had been cheating or had someone else pregnant? Was he going to leave me?

BTS:
I looked at him, waiting to hear what he had to say.

"Mag, I love you and will always love you. Let's get up early Sunday morning and go to church."

I started crying tears of joy because I just knew he was going to say something terrible. He held me tight the rest of the way home. The cab ride seemed like it was three hours in my mind. It was only forty minutes.

I am tired
I have done things that
Were not illegal, but
Really wrong
My thought process was sick
My visions are awful
Fulfilling my own selfish needs
Has become my number one habit
I am addicted to myself
My feelings for anyone besides
Myself have dwindled
I have never put these thoughts
On paper before
But now I want
Healing
So God please come
And get me because
I am tired of
Living like this
In Jesus' name
I pray — Amen
Amen Amen

It was Sunday morning. We were sitting in church. I was like a child because it had been so long since I had been here. I didn't even know what to do. But, I liked how I felt there. I felt like God was in the present, not just someone we wished for. The choir stood, and they were the old folks. So, I assumed it was the senior choir. Their first song was one of my favorites; my grandmother used to play it every Sunday and when times were hard, like someone died, etc. — "I didn't Feel No Ways Tired" by Reverend James Cleveland. Immediately, I started feeling some kind of way, and when the choir belted, *"I have come so far from where I started from/I didn't believe he bought me this far to leave me,"* I started crying. I was on my feet, singing every verse of that song. I couldn't control myself. Raymond stood beside me and he and I sung and cried. I started to confess to God silently: *Please, please forgive me because I have sinned. I have done too many things wrong to mention. Dear Heavenly Father, please accept my apologies, in Jesus' name I pray. Amen. Amen. Amen.*

From that moment, it was like a peace came over me. I had never felt like that before. It was scary yet soothing. I also felt at peace; didn't know what peace was but, I felt it. I was still crying like a baby, but, I sensed relief; released from all the pain I was feeling, released from all the pain I created, released from just everything. I really didn't know what else to do. I didn't realize this, but, I was so overcome with emotion, I fainted.

Pause: At that point, I didn't know who was telling the story. I think some would call it the Holy Ghost or even the angels.

BTS:

I finally came to, and I was lying in the back pew. The choir was singing my other favorite song—"I Feel Like Going On." As the angelic voiced in the choir sung, *"I feel like going on. Times may be tough. Trials come on every hand. But I feel like, I feel like going on,"* stirred something inside me, and I felt like I could go on. I was crying again. This church stuff was getting good. I would start coming every Sunday. I might even get saved.

Pause: Let me hold up on the saved part until I get that Christian walk right.

BTS:

I really love that church stuff. I didn't know why I had not been in so long. Maybe it was because it also scared me. I didn't want people to look at me differently or judge me. Church folk tended to be the most critical. They judged how the others walked, talked, and especially how they dressed. So I would hold up on getting saved until I got that thing together. As service was still going on, the pastor finally stepped up to the pulpit. He could sing also, picking up where the choir left off. I felt like going on. Those trials may come and go, but I feel like going on. I was crying again. The pastor sounded like James Cleveland. He was tearing up that song. The choir was back on their feet. Everyone in the church was singing. Even the ushers felt it. That was an incredible experience. It all settled down. Now the pastor started to preach. I still remember the sermon. The title was, "How to Live Holy." He was speaking on the principle of how to live holy in God's eye not in man's eye. We were always trying to live for man instead of God. As humans, we need to stop that. He went into detail about how man cannot save you, but God can. How man will always fail you and God will never let you down. So do as God states in the Bible and stop listening to man. Then he gave a personal testimony about having faith and listening to God and doing His will.

"You will not change all at once—a little at a time—then you will know you are doing God's work. So don't make it hard on yourself. You did not start all of your sins in one day. It took some time. So it will also take time to heal them," the pastor preached.

I yelled, "Preach, pastor! Preach, pastor!"

People turned around and looked at me. I didn't care anymore about what people thought of me. I had been a people-pleaser all my life. Now I needed to start living for God even if I didn't know how yet. It seemed like we had been in church for three to six hours, but it had really only been two and one-half hours. I really felt so strange, but good at the same time. Service was over. We were walking out hand-in-hand. We got in the Benz and headed to breakfast. At breakfast, we talked about our life together and the children and just getting closer to God. I think this was the changing point in my life.

Church
A place I stay far away from
Did not know if it was fear
Or just scared to commit
Church
I know it's a good place
Grandma and mom always talk good
About it
Church
Its one on every corner
They do all sorts of good things
For the community
Church
So why don't I go
To see what's going on
Church
I will answer that right now
I am going back to
Church

BTS:

Raymond and I were still discussing church over breakfast. We actually held hands as we prayed before we ate. These were new thoughts for me. I told Raymond that next week I wanted the girls to go with us, and I also wanted him to stop working on Sundays. My mother always said that was the Lord's Day. But, honor Him. No work or chores — just praise Him and have family time.

Pause: I am starting to sound like my mother. It's funny how you despise someone when you are younger, then as an adult you actually start acting and looking like them — good and bad.

BTS:

I really needed to call and see my mother. I blamed a whole lot of my bad decisions in life on her. She never abused me or hurt me. I just felt that she could have helped to prevent me from making all the foolish mistakes I made. Time has truly healed my wounds and, of course, God. I would pray all the time. But, at one time, I did not think God listened to me. But, He really does. God has revealed all of my faults. The reason I had been losing sleep, the reason behind my stress was because I had been looking for a manmade miracle. How could I get over what was going on with me? All I ever needed, God has for me. So, why was I tripping?

Dear God,
I realize all I need
All I ever wanted is in you
You are everything
And everything is you
From my sleepless nights
To my ho'ing days
Just knowing that you care
Creates so much joy
Inside my brittle heart

Dear God,
I want to stop running
I have been scared of hurting again
I want a good life for my girls
I know I have not been
The best mother, wife, or friend

Dear God,
Please heal me and
Let me be better
In Jesus' name I pray
Amen-Amen-Amen

BTS:

I told Raymond my thoughts of wanting to see my mother and grandmother.

"I wondered why you were so distant from them and don't even let the girls visit," he said.

I told Raymond I had some deep hurts I was dealing with. Now lately, I have been feeling like I needed to let them go and after church today, I knew I really needed to clean that part of my life.

Raymond asked, "Did someone hurt or molest you physically?"

"No." But at times my hurt was so deep; it felt like someone was touching me.

Raymond asked me again, "Was someone touching or molesting you?"

"No."

"Look, Margaret, you need to get over it or get counseling. But, I suggest you take it to the Lord. He can heal any wound."

Pause: A man that prays – wow – this was new to me. I always thought men were too strong to pray. I never saw a man pray besides the pastor. Church was filled with women and a few men. A man that prays...that has to be the door to heaven. My husband started talking in an unknown language. Later I learned it was tongues, meaning he was in conversation with the Lord. A man that prays — at that moment, I was just in worship because it was so powerful to see — a man that prays.

BTS:
We finally arrived home. I went next door to pick up the girls. When I get to the door, I saw our neighbor, Al.

"Come on in, Maggie," he said. I proceed with caution. "Sit down for a spell."

"Al, where are Renee and Rojena?"

"They are with my wife and kids at the mall. They should be gone for about three hours."

"Okay. I will be back then."

The next thing I know, he had the front door closed and he was under my dress.

Pause: That caught me totally off guard.

BTS:
"Al, stop playing! Al!" Before I knew it, he was licking sweetness and all the oceans surrounding it. I was enjoying it until thoughts of church popped in my head. I forcefully pushed him off which made him come back harder.

"Oh, Maggie, you didn't like it anymore?" he yelled.

"No," I said, even though he was one of the best coochie eaters in the world.

New thoughts
I have to have them
All the things I knew before
Have to change
New thoughts
This will be the hardest training
That I have ever had
How to rethink everything I know
To think of others also
New thoughts
I am going to finish
This poem when I actually have
New thoughts

BTS:
So, Al and I were fussing now. He was trying to manhandle me. I started stealing him in the face. He swung back. I wound up and hit him with three punches to the chin and one directly in his nose. His nose started bleeding. Blood was running down

his face onto the front of his shirt. It was running like water and he started to pick me up. I grabbed the lamp and smashed his head, and he was still holding me. I was kicking him.

"Let me go!!" I screamed, not realizing how loud I had said it.

I heard noise, sounding like someone knocked the damn door down. I looked up and it was Raymond. Al's eyes looked like they would pop out of his head. I was just looking because I was not sure what was about to happen. I looked in Raymond's eyes and I could not see him. It was like some demon had possessed him. I started praying:

Dear God,
It's me Maggie
I know I don't deserve to be saved
But I don't think I deserve to die either
Rojena and Renee need their mother
I need my husband
Please God stop this nonsense that I created
In Jesus' name I pray
Amen-Amen-Amen

BTS:
Within minutes the commotion stopped. Raymond grabbed my hand and we walked out of there hand-in-hand.

Freeze: I heard prayer changes all things. But that was quick!

BTS:
We walked back to the house. We sat on the loveseat and he hugged me tight. I embraced him and we started crying.

Pause: All I could think about was that O'Jays' song "We Cried Together."

BTS:
Our embrace was not only physical. I felt his heart kind of touching his soul. I had never felt that feeling before. We didn't talk about what went on with Al. The next thing I knew, we were upstairs butt naked in the bedroom. He was sitting on my face. I was demolishing his ass. My tongue was so far up in him, he was screaming and creaming like me. Once I finished licking his ass, I looked up on the ceiling and realized that his orgasm was

so strong that it was now on the ceiling, dripping. Damn! That was powerful. Cum on the ceiling...

We continued to please each other until I heard footsteps coming up the stairs.

"Raymond, put your clothes on," I yelled.

He puts on some shorts. I grabbed a nightgown. The bedroom door was wide open. The footsteps got closer. It was Rojena and Renee.

"Hey, Mommy."

"Hi, Daddy."

"How are y'all doing?"

"Did you enjoy your night out? Did y'all see Mr. Santoas' face? Somebody beat his butt."

We both started laughing uncontrollably.

Rojena asked, "Mommy, what's so funny?"

"Baby, it's a joke between your father and me."

Renee said, "Mommy, let us in on the joke. We like a good laugh."

"It's one of those jokes you have to be grown up to understand."

Rojena chimed in. "There they go again with that adult stuff."

Now we are all laughing. I tell them to leave the room so their father and I can get some clothes on. They walked out and closed the door.

Raymond said, "We are not putting no damn clothes on. We are going to finish what you started."

I grab my Fisherman cough drops from the night stand, bent over and started deep-throating his manhood. He eased me up a little so he could touch my sweetness. I did not know he had his own plan. I thought he was just going to feel on my clit.

Pause: Men — Learn how to slowly manipulate the clit without damaging it or being too rough or brutal.

BTS:
I thought that was his plan. But he had a gadget I had never seen before. My eyes got so big you would have thought I had seen a ghost. That equipment was freaking me out. It was shaped like a man's piece, but it had other gadgets coming from it. He slipped it in me and just the entry made me cum. Then he turned it on. It made all my bells and whistles go off in my body. I was no good. So since he was pleasing me and I was going out of my way to please him even more, I stopped deep-throating and did my patented swirl motion around the head of his manhood. He was enjoying that a little too much. But, for real, I liked to see him enjoy himself. It made my enjoyment and fulfillment even better.

This was why I have sex. I liked to see others enjoy themselves. That's why I was a people-pleaser. But, along the way, I learned how to also enjoy myself. Not just alone, but with anyone I decided to have sex with. He turned on another gadget. On that one mechanism, that piece went up my ass. It was now in both of my special places at one time.

Pause: Nicknames — I have told you numerous times, my pussy were called "sweetness" and "lips the gripper." I also have a name for my ass. It's called "nicety" because you have to be really nice to me in order to enter that wonderful place.

BTS:

Once he entered Nicety, it totally froze up all my emotions and my body for about five minutes. I had to adjust in my body and my mind. My body because Nicety was tight. My mind because this was totally taboo — even though I do it. Everything in society has programmed us on how bad this was and the kind of person you are when you do what I was doing and enjoyed it. I loved it. It was what really got me off. I have had more multi-Os from Nicety than anywhere else on my body. So as I said before, I loved it.

Nicety
Here it is. That place
Others only dream of
The place on entry that people dare
To explore
Some would call no-man's land
Others ask, you do that?
Nicety
The few that know its worth
Would say yes and can I be next
Society has condemned it
All your friends think you are bold
Some would call you nasty or a freak
Nicety
Others want to explore
Some are just scared
Some would actually call it
Taboo

BTS:

As the intensity of all that action started to fulfill every crevice and every thought in my vivid imagination, I embraced Raymond and told him he was the best man I had ever known. He stopped screwing my ass and embraced me. We hugged each other into the night. This was the most wonderful experience I had ever had. It was totally mesmerizing. I was laying there hoping I didn't die. I was not in pain. I had never felt that complete in my entire life. Totally fulfilled, so content, so real, this was just not true. What was going on? Now I was starting to question everything. How did I come through life and never felt that way? From my mother, my grandmother, or any man? The only time I ever felt totally complete was when I was in church. I started to cry and wondered if this was heaven on earth.

Yonder

Heaven on Earth
A place where there are
Only tears of joy
A place only few have
Ever experienced
A place and time
That mirrors all eternity
Will we meet our maker there?
Or will it be that Glorious Day
When we are no longer
On Earth

The End

Stay tuned for part VI of
"Maggie's Madness"
in *Taboo 6*.

Feenin'

Trying to do and be someone that was always trying to stay out of trouble, along the way, the mischief and the deceit had ruined all my relationships, including my family. I tried twelve-step programs. I tried abstinence. I even tried to relieve myself. But each trial seemed like an error because my conditions worsened. I even had thoughts of suicide. But, of course, that one was the least-explored because, if anything, Mr. Roarke sure loved himself. But what was I to do? Almost met my death twice. Was I a cat with nine lives or was that my time to finally fulfill my life's mission? I would say yes if I knew my mission. Could it be just a coincidence that I was still here? At one time in my life, I would agree. But, as I got older and just a little bit wiser, I realized that nothing was coincidence. Coincidence was God's way of letting woman or man take the credit. So that was another theory out the window. So to get some agreement, I would PUSH — pray until something happened.

How could that be? Someone tried to kill me, again. Only a cat had nine lives. I didn't want to live like this. But for some unknown reason, this was the place where I always ended up.

Recap: for the last year, someone has tried to kill me. First, I was shot by a drive-by shooting that blew out all the windows in the car and holes in all the doors. When I left the hospital, someone tried to strangle me until Dre rescued me before they tried to throw me off the balcony. There was at least one other incident that could have been deadly. I had been beaten unconscious and left for dead.

BTS:

I was trying to figure out what to do or if I should just move out of town. I was asked to move my company to New York, but would that solve my problem? If I couldn't control myself in the DMV (Washington, DC, Maryland, Virginia), I knew I would lose my mind in the tri-state (New York, New Jersey, Connecticut) down the street from Canada. I would probably lose my mind there, too — maybe even my life. But for real, I didn't want to leave my mother. Yes I was a ho'. But really, I'm a mamma's boy. I love me some Rojena. When she was sick, I was sick. When she would hurt, I would hurt. It had been that way since I was a baby.

Pause: When I was in kindergarten, my mother took me to downtown Washington, DC. We were at the counter at a major department store. We both got deathly sick. The doctor had to come to our house to treat us. (That's when doctors made house calls.) Since then, even when we were not physically together, we were sick at the same time. As an adult, my mother would call me and ask me if I was sick because she was and as usual, she was right.

BTS:
But, I was really considering moving or just getting a place in New York. First, I had to convince my mother that this was a wise choice. I didn't think I mentioned this, but my mother was Chief Operating Office of my consulting firm. All business decisions I made were with her and most decisions that affected my future, I discussed with her. I didn't always take her advice. But I did talk to her about them. One thing I was sure of, I needed to start talking to God before I got into crazy positions, instead of calling Him once someone was trying to kill me.

Pause: Always at the other side on each occasion, I was on the receiving end. I have had my ass whipped more this year than any time in my life. I had been so unsure of myself and the direction of my company and my spirituality. I wanted to get saved. But would that really change me and all the foolishness that came with being a true Gemini? Yes, there were at least one hundred personalities in my mind. I only had control of ten of them. The other ninety had to fend for themselves. I wanted to say they're the ones that got me in trouble, but I was trying not to lie. The ten that I knew real well were the personalities that were always doing dirt along with being money-hungry and deceitful. Five of them were total hos. So as we continue to explore those, I will end with why I was always on the other side. But I know because I created it. Always at the other side.

BTS:

I needed to search for a love of my own. Someone that not only understood me sexually, but, someone that was so intellectual that when my thoughts were so expressive that she could actually intimidate me mentally, which was the biggest turn on; someone that could get in my mind versus my pants. If I ever found that woman, I would stop all my nonsense and marry her. I think all of my life would then change. I wanted to have children and a normal life. I wanted someone who loved me like my mother did. No one loved me like that. They say there was no stronger love than a mother and son. I truly believed that statement. My mother actually loved me during good days and prayed for me during trying times. I was tripping—emotionally, physically, and definitely sexually. I was truly a recovering ho'. I guess I couldn't be a recovering ho' until I admitted that I had a problem.

My. name is Courtney Edwards and I was a ho'. I had so much fornication that most humans couldn't even imagine having that much sex in their entire lifetime. I had done it with so many people, in so many places, I couldn't even figure out how many people I have actually had sex with or the number of times. Nor did I even know them all—from the one-night-stands to the many relationships to the massive cheating. But I am not bragging. If I was younger, I would have been. But since I matured just a bit, I was just blessed that I didn't have herpes or AIDS and my piece still worked good. So in that regard, I was thankful. Also, I didn't have any children from all those bad decisions because I never wore rubbers or took any precautions. So I knew it was just God.

Foolish Behavior
We all have done it
As youth and some still
As we turned older
Foolish Behavior
As a young man I lived on that street
As I got older remained there
Sometimes enjoyed it
Thought I was having fun
Foolish Behavior
Sometimes we never stop
As adults, we revel in it
Also, we justify our behavior
Foolish Behavior
We even convince our friends
To behave the same way
Also push this on our children
Especially our boys
Foolish Behavior
Sadly society condones
This situation and glamourizes it
Foolish Behavior
When does it end
It's totally up to a boy

Finally becoming a man
And accepting responsibility
No longer defining his existence
With his dick

BTS:

I was referring to a man. But the real reason I was a ho' was because women had allowed me to be one. Just being nice, as most would call a gentleman, and lifting their self-esteem with compliments from how smart they were to their financial stability. And the kicker was letting them know how much better they were from the other women I'd dated, which also gave me a chance to know up front what I didn't tolerate. For example:

Tell her something like "I can't stand women with drama" so she would never come around you when there was an issue that might involve drama.

Another one of my favorites was "I can't stand women that curse or act rough." That would get her sweet-talking, always looking and acting like a lady. It was totally a mind game. If I got your mind, I have everything that your mind controlled from your body to your car to your time and, of course, your finances.

BTS:

It was Sunday morning. I was on my way to church. This was the same church I went to a while back. It was in southeast Washington, DC, and a whole lot of folks that grew up with me in Barry Farms went there — from old drug dealers to the old players and hos. So I was in good company; not too lost by myself. As I walked into the place of Glory, tears were streaming down my face like an inner peace resonating in my soul — something I had been yearning. I had never been that complacent since I was a little boy hugged up in my mother's arms. I felt like someone was holding me tightly saying, *My child, welcome home.*

Pause: I started to think about the numerous passages I read from the Bible. There was on passage I read all the time — Luke 15:33. The passage is about the prodigal son. To break it down, it about two sons, one got his share of money from his father, left town and spent it foolishly on alcohol and women. He was a biblical ho'. After blowing all his money, he went to work in someone's pig pens, while eating and living like the pigs. He finally swallowed his pride and returned to his father's farm to work for him because he knew he had disappointed his father. So as he got close to his father's farm, his father saw him coming and sent the farmhands to run and get him, clean him up and to slaughter the fattest pig because they were having a feast. His long lost son was back. The prodigal son had squandered all his wealth and his father greeted him back with opened arms.

This was the question I never heard anyone ask. What happened to the other son? Did he leave? Did he get jealous? Could someone at least answer that for me?

BTS:

Sometimes I felt like the prodigal son because it was time to come home. I didn't know where home was. I didn't know a whole lot of things about myself. I wanted to do some research on my background. I knew my father. But, I didn't know a lot about his background. His mother, who was my grandmother, never married. He had one sister, who he took care of when my grandmother died. Once she was grown, she moved to California and no one had seen her since. I don't think he knew who his father was. I knew he attended DC Public Schools, but never graduated and was an altar boy at the Catholic Church by RFK Stadium. He loved that church. This was also the same church that he took me and my brother, Shake, to on Sundays.

This was when they still spoke in Latin. After church, we would go to his aunt's house and sit on her furniture with the plastic coverings that stuck to our backs. We would stay there for hours. I actually miss those days when people would stop over your house for hours just to talk. As a society, we have gotten so far from that—just talking. I needed some rest. Once I start talking about my past, I would get emotionally drained. I don't know if it's because of the emotions or if it was that there was something there I feared or wanted to hide. I don't think it was that I didn't know what was in my past. So I sure didn't know what to hide. I felt like I had not slept in months. I felt so restless, just anxious all at the same time.

These feelings
All of a sudden new thoughts
New seasons new feelings
Feelings of spacyness
Which means I am lost
Because sometimes I don't
Feel like I am even on
This earth
These feelings
Lost, gone, searching and stuck
Is how I would describe it
Distant, close and just gone off the deep end
Is where I have been
These feelings
No longer feel independent
Just drained and emotionally
Unavailable
These feelings

BTS:

I knew it was time to go to sleep now because I felt like I was babbling. My words were losing its meaning. I was getting further off course and all my emotions were coming up. I was starting to have thoughts of everything good and bad that went on

in my childhood. I was walking to my bedroom.
As I got into my bed, I say a prayer:

Dear God,
It's me the fool again
I am weak, anxious, and feeling
Real low right now
Please change these thoughts and
My actions
In Jesus' name I pray
Amen-Amen-Amen

I was sleeping for about fifteen minutes before
my body shook and woke me up. I was having
more thoughts of my childhood. So I knew what
to do.

Pause: Long baths – I love taking baths. It has always
soothed all my ailments in my mind.

BTS:
So, I ran bath water. As I was waiting for the water
to fill up the tub, it was like a cleansing affect, like
my soul was being purified. All the mess that was
in me felt like it was purging. I don't know a whole
lot of scriptures, but that did feel spiritual. There

I go again with that Jesus stuff. So as the water continued to flow, my tears started to flow.

Pause: Damn, I have cried more this month than I have in my entire life.

BTS:

It was time for me to man up and get through all the fears of heartbreak, abandonment, lack of a male role model, lack of love. At times, anything that miss or thought I was missing, I needed to get over it. It was time to become a faultless man. I had never seen one, but I wanted to become one. I finally got in the tub. It was all bubbly and I loved it.

Pause: You are reading correctly. I love bubble baths and yes I'm straight.

BTS:

I turned on the radio and a song I never wanted to hear came on—"I Don't Want To Lose You" by Phyllis Hyman. Now I was about to lose it. But I held on and sung along. She started to get into the part where she sung, *"I want to lose you. I love you just the way you are. I couldn't love you more."* It was like

God was saying those words to me. But I wondered how God could love like I was. I was a ho'. I was no good. I only cared about myself. Besides not lying to my mother, I lied to everyone else and God still wanted me. I started to reminisce about a song my mother used to listen to on Saturday mornings as we cleaned the house.

Side note: Does every family in America get up early on Saturdays to clean up the entire house?

BTS:
"Goin' Up Yonder" by Walter Hawkins and The Love Center Choir was that memorable song. As I enjoyed the soothing bubble bath, I reminisced on the lyrics: *I am goin' up yonder to be with my Lord.* Each time I heard that song, it was like I was taking off, going there. I guess yonder was Heaven. I sure wanted to go and leave this bad earth. *Goin' up yonder to be with my Lord.* I was really into that song. But it was like a movement. I wanted to stay there forever. Sometimes I wish I could. Then other times, I realized I actually do love living. So I would stay. All these feelings of wanting to be here overwhelmed me. Then that song came back in my head — "I Don't Want To Lose You." I couldn't help

but sing the lyrics, *"Who do you think you are? Who do you want to be?"* I was just floored by these words. I didn't know how to answer. All of a sudden, I really didn't understand. It was that time when you were just in awe and didn't know what to say or do. So I just started to pray. My mother used to say when you didn't know what to do, just pray. So I got on my knees.

Dear God,
Guess who? Yes it's me
For the millionth time
Seeking your face
Seeking your time
Seeking to know that
I am still important to you
It was my heart, soul, mind
And body that I am in
Need of healing
I am lost, confused, crazy
And just tired
Please just give me some directions

In Jesus' name I pray
Amen-Amen-Amen

BTS:

I started feeling somewhat like myself. I started to think rationally. I had come up with an epiphany: If God had planned for me to be gone, I would already be gone. Remember I had been shot, beaten and left for dead. So I guess it was not time. Why would He keep me around? It was beyond my ability to get all spiritual and deep, so I will not even fake like I know. But one thing I did know was that I planned to enjoy the time I did have left. The first thing I planned to do was spend some quality time with my mother. I had truly neglected her these last few months. I had been a ho' gone wild. How could I let a body part destroy all that I had worked for?

Pause: Sadly, a whole lot of wars are started and more than a few people killed for the same reasons. Men and women get so engrossed into another's life; they feel like they are one. If it is only one way, the other does not return the affection. This is when the drama starts on both sides.

BTS:

I was at that place numerous times. Most recently was when I was with Tessa. I would do anything for her and it still was not good enough. I was getting better as a man every day and she still rejected me.

Pause: Rejection – hurts almost as much as being shot and beaten because it is eternal. There is nothing to cure. There is no medicine or bandages and you can't sleep it away. It is even worse when you are younger because you never think you are going to recover.

Flashback:

When I was sixteen, I fell for a young lady that I stayed with for five years. She broke my heart so badly. I am still recuperating after almost seven years. We did everything together. She was my first everything, including my first heartache. I felt so badly about her after our breakup. Then she would torture me once a year by coming back on New Year's Eve. They say whoever you are with on New Year's Eve you will be with them for the rest of your life. That was the biggest lie that anyone could ever tell because after she would come into my life on that day, she would sex my brains out and leave. I would not hear from her until that time the following year. So never believe or tell that lie again.

BTS:

After reliving that flashback, I realized why I am like I am. I blamed most of it on my father, but I have some of my own issues, which I had never wanted to admit to. Now tears were streaming down my face. I had forgotten about that memory. Maybe I suppressed it so that I would not have to take the blame myself. I guess I was really maturing, admitting that I was part of my problem. After that pain from her, I should have gone to church or a psychologist.

Pause: I know you are saying black folks don't go to psychologists. But if we did, we would be better as a whole instead of making our issues generational. Someone has to break the cycle of destruction, hurts, egos, ho-ism, and all the other vices that come with not facing a problem.

BTS:

Since I never received counseling or went to church at the time, I made all others suffer the wrath of Mr. Roarke and whatever else I inherited from my father, which of course my brother has these issues as well. If we don't break the chain, our children will have the same issues. So I am trying to break that cycle. I have known many women that suffered from these symptoms. I was starting to realize my childish, immature ways and wanted to put them behind me and be a better person. But how do I become a better person overnight? I didn't think it would happen that fast, but I was going to try. Now this was another task that I had added to the things I wanted to accomplish soon. Hopefully, I was not dreaming again or just wishing on a star. I tried not to dream or wish too much because I was a realist. I believed that the things that were already ordained to happen to me — good, bad or indifferent — would happen, as much as I thought I was the cat with nine lives. A list of all the changes that have occurred was just a piece of my own sick sense of reality. My attitude for the ladies was totally insatiable. This was an addiction. Admittedly, I truly have a problem. But, was there a class for sexual addiction or sexual satisfaction? That was the only thing I could call it. Or, could I say I was addicted to orgasms? So that would make me an O-chaser. Chasing after orgasms all my life because I liked to cum. But, it had to be deeper than that. But for real, being a man, as most men know, we are really not that deep.

Example: Men need women's approval more than anyone else. That is why we always lying about how big our "Johnsons" are and how long we can last.

BTS:

Most men are just average with special skills. We are not that deep. We are as shallow as a bowl of Jell-O or pudding. As I get older, I want to be deeper. I am well-read and have taken numerous college courses. With a few more classes, I will have my degree.

The water in the tub was starting to get cold. But I heard noises in my living room. Someone just came through the door. It must be Dre or my mother. Those were the only two people with keys. So I ran some hot water and sat for a little while longer. I was assuming that either Dre or my mother would knock on the door. After about ten minutes I started to get anxious—actually nervous. They should have at least hollered my name by now. I pulled the drain plug for the water to drain. As I was getting out of the tub, someone barged through the door. I grabbed the towel to cover myself. But it was too late. They dropped a hot iron in the tub. I jumped out of the tub just in time, hitting my head on the toilet. Blood was gushing out like a faucet.

Pause: I pause in my own mind. This cannot be happening again. This time, I am going to be the one that will not get hurt.

BTS:
So, I am butt naked, fighting that unknown attacker who wore a ski mask and all black. I got out of the bathroom and held on to the door long enough to put on some shorts. I released the door. It swung open and I started throwing punches. Then I thought to grab the TV. I grabbed it and threw it in his chest. Now he was on the floor. I didn't want to kill him. So I let them get up.

Pause: I am too scared of jail to kill anyone.

BTS:
He finally got the TV off him and started backing up. I was so pumped up; I started swinging again and again until he was almost unconscious. Then I do that move I saw the Chinese folks do in karate movies. I did a roundhouse kick. Shit! I surprised myself. I caught him off guard, which knocked

him off his feet. He started talking, but I couldn't understand what he was saying. But, I recognized the voice. I blocked out the voice and pulled the person off the floor, and out, closing the door. I was pumped. I could fight a whole army right now. I locked the door and put the chain on and started to pray. But it was a "mad" prayer.

Damn!
It's happening again
Someone is after me
Someone is trying to kill me again
Damn!
Here it is I am no longer
Breaking hearts
I am trying to live right
Damn!
I am even treating people better
And trying to stop hurting people
Yes I am still selfish
And it's always about me
Damn!
But I am working on it
You never said I had to
Change everything all at once
Damn!
I am going to try harder
And harder because this i
A task I can't fail
Damn!

BTS:

I knew I needed to see my mother, but I didn't feel like being chastised nor did I want to be banned from the house. My mother loved me so much. Sometimes she would ban me from coming over her house if she felt my spirit was not right. She knew it would never be pure, but she at least wanted me to be working on things. I called Dre and got no answer. I called Shake. I got no answer. I was getting anxious again. The three folks that always had my back were nowhere to be found. Now I was actually scared. I needed to stay somewhere secretive for a while. I needed to get out of the limelight. Just maybe, New York was not a bad idea after all. I knew I was out of my mind now because I didn't plan to tell anyone where I was going.

I packed up some things and went to the hotel up the street from my house. Next to the hotel was a club called Triples where the Go-Go bands played. I checked in and went to sleep. About 11:30 p.m., I woke up because I heard people in the parking lot. Then I realized there was a Go-Go tonight. It was Rare Essence. They were my favorite. I got dressed and went down to the club. They had already started, so it was a full fledge party. Weed smoke was everywhere. Drinks were flowing. And of course the ladies and fellas were lined up against the walls. I was truly in my element. I went up front because I knew the band and spoke to everyone. As I started dancing, the band called out my name.

Pause: Go-Go — if you are not from the DMV — Washington, DC, Maryland, Virginia — you would not understand it. Go-Go is a group of people that perform a type of music derived from drums and congas mixed with keyboards and guitars, with call and response from the person on the microphone. You have to experience it in person to understand.

BTS:
As I was enjoying myself, I could feel it. But I wanted to deny it. The zone was creeping up around me. Actually it started taking over me in the room and all I could do was represent it and embrace it. The honeys started to notice it and it was on all over again. I was the main event, the main attraction. When you looked for me, you looked for action. So I just embraced the zone and decided to enjoy it for the night since I was leaving town tomorrow. Who knew when or if I would get to see Rare Essence

again? I was going to miss this town. But I needed a break and I just might die here and die soon. I started to enjoy myself. I went to the bar and got me a drink—Bacardi and Coke—because I wanted to get drunk, but not horny. Gin made me horny. I got my drink, tipped the bartender, and I was back on the floor. Essence was tearing the place up. I gulped my down drink because I was ready to get my dance on. It was a honey in front of me. I start dancing behind her. She turned around and started moving up toward me. I really wanted to dance alone. But she got closer and closer. So it was on. Rare Essence started singing, *"Shake what you brought with you 'cause you know what it's gonna get ya."* Every honey was shaking that butt like they were invitations to get it. So the honey that I was dancing with started putting it on me. I was trying to be respectful. But it was getting the best of me. I held out for about three minutes. Now it was on! I was all up on her, enjoying myself. I loved the Go-Go. Then they went into the song "Freaks Come Out At Night." Damn! That was my theme song. I started to sing along, "That's right—freaks come out—freaks come out at night." I was enjoying this.

The honey turned around and said, "Don't I know you?"

"I didn't think so."

"I have seen you somewhere before. What is your name?"

"Courtney."

"For real? Well you must have a twin. It is a dude named Roarke that lives in SE that looks just like you."

"Never heard of him." I changed the subject and asked her if she would like a drink.

She said, "Let's finish out this beat first."

She started to get low and started freaking me. So we both were singing, "That's right the freaks come out—the freaks come out at night."

I could not have planned that better—a freak on the song "Freaks Come Out at Night." Then she turned around and let me ride her and now I was up on her like a pickle on a peppermint stick. So after about fifteen minutes, the band shouted, "Let's slow it down."

As much as I wanted to get off the dance floor, she said, "Let's dance off of this slow song."

The band played a song by O'Brien called "Lady I Love You." I was not in love. But it was certain songs that took me there. And that was that song. As I held her tight, every memory of Tessa, my mother, and every other woman that I truly loved started to surface. It was all coming back, but I refused to cry again. So as we were on the floor grinding, I tried to block my emotions because I was tired of crying. So I got back into her. While we were dancing, I asked her for her name.

"Shayla."

"Well that is different."

"Shut up. Get closer and let me feel you."

So I did just that. I was so close; I could feel every fiber of her emotions. She could probably hear each beat of my heart. It was pumping so hard, I felt like it was getting older by the minute. My heart never pumped that hard.

Everything must change
I need to grow up
Stop being the man I used to be
Walk in authority
And stand for something
Having sex does not need
To be number one anymore
Helping people and supporting my family
Have been my priority
Doing business above the table
And not in the bedroom
Everything must change
To grow up to be a respected
Gentleman and a businessman
Of integrity
Not fulfilling my own selfishness
And helping others to realize
These dreams and visions are
Where I stand
I have to stop talking
About God and start
Walking with him
Everything must change

BTS:

I continued to slow dance. It seemed like both of us were in a trance as if our souls were connected. I just met her. But it seemed deeper than that. I looked in her eyes. I realized I didn't know her. But I still felt that instant intimacy. It kind of scared me, but I wanted to explore it. So the song was ending after what seemed like three hours. I grabbed her hand and took her to the bar. I just ordered two Rum and Cokes, paid the bartender, and we went and sat down. No words were spoken — just stares and touches. We were stroking each other's face, neck, and palms. Then we embrace tightly. Out of nowhere, we were hugging. It was as if she could read my mind. I looked at her again to make sure I really had not been with her before. I liked this feeling. But I was curious as to why she knew so much of how to manage my thoughts and moves.

Maybe I know her
She knows how to manage me
In thoughts and moves
Talking to her is so soothing
Touching her feels like silk to my hands
Her scent smells familiar
It is comforting to be around her
I want to explore her
I want to keep this feeling
I like this feeling and this girl
Where do I go from here
And is this a trick
Is someone setting me up
As I said before
Maybe I know her

BTS:

We started to talk. She asked me, "Courtney, what are you doing the rest of the night?" I was dumbfounded because those were my thoughts. I was gonna ask her the same thing. Now I just let her lead. "My girlfriends and I have a room in the hotel. We are having an after party."

Pause: As much as I wanted to go, I knew it was not a good idea. I didn't know that girl and I was starting to think with the head inside my pants. I guess I was growing up.

BTS:

I tell her "No."

She then asked could she come to my room. I wanted to say no, but I needed some pussy before I left town. I decided to get that last piece of in-town pussy, so I agreed that she could come to my room. We left Triples Nightclub and I led her to my room, which was attached to the club. It was an ingenious idea to attach a night club to a hotel.

She said, "Let me tell my girlfriend first."

I pulled her in closer to me, and said, "No."

She looked puzzled, but followed me anyway.

Pause: I told her no because I didn't want any drama. No visitors tonight.

BTS:
So as we started to walk to the room, I saw some familiar faces. But they didn't see me because I needed to disappear completely. I picked up the pace and as I was walking, I was already figuring out how I was going to turn her inside out. This would be the best she will ever have. I planned to leave her in the room unconscious, babbling like a baby. We walked through the back way to get to the room. I opened the door and we went in.

"Can I use the bathroom?" she asked.

"Yeah," I said, nodding.

I turned on the TV and made us some drinks. I heard water running in the bathroom. So I sat back and relaxed. In about eight minutes, she opened the door. I had my back turned. I was making another drink. When I turned around, what I saw did not startle me or surprise me. But it sure looked good. She came out of the bathroom butt naked, water glistening on of her body. It was a most beautiful sight. I had visions of all the beautiful ladies I had been with. So I got lost in deep thought for almost ten minutes. I had been with so many beauties,

I tried to stay in pause so I could enjoy. She was still standing there glistening. Then she got one of the drinks and just continued to look in my eyes. For some strange reason, I couldn't move. It was like I was frozen in time. I saw her, but, I couldn't touch her. I smelled her sweet scent, but I was just paralyzed. I couldn't move a finger. So I was not sure what to do next. Finally the temporary frozen moment in time ended. I moved toward her beautiful body. As I moved closer, I thought before I ventured. So I moved toward my duffle bag first. I got out my box of Magnums.

Pause: Magnums are an upgrade of condoms — meant to fit a Black man or any man that packing and the sensitivity is amazing. It feels like going in raw.

BTS:
So I grabbed my bag and turned it over. "Man, they must be at the bottom."

"What are you looking for?"

"Condoms."

"Please — you don't need them. I am clean."

Pause: You cannot tell by looking at someone that they have a STD. For real, the times I got a STD, it was from someone that was drop dead gorgeous. So don't believe the hype. Use protection or don't do it.

BTS:
"Naw, baby, I've gotta find my condoms before we get busy."

She walked over to me and started kissing me, and undressing me. This was feeling good, but I couldn't function until I found the rubbers. She completely pulled off my clothes. So we were both butt naked. I still couldn't proceed because I refused to go in raw. I was getting weak, but I was determined not to do it raw. She started dancing as if she was a stripper — very seductive. I just watched, turned on — but cautious. My mind started to wander. *Did I put the condoms in the bag at all?* I got up off the bed and went back into my bag. I had to find those condoms. I pulled everything out on the floor.

She yelled, "Come on and get this pussy or are you scared? If you scared, say you scared!"

Pause: Six months ago, I would have just jumped in raw. Who she think she is saying I am scared? I am Mr. Roarke. I ain't scared of nothing or no one. Now I'm pissed.

BTS:

I was mad, but not too mad to do something that foolish. After turning the bag inside out, I saw the condoms on the floor. As I rolled one on, I was excited because I was about to turn that place out. I planned to do her so good; she would be looking for me the rest of her life.

Pause: That's my ego talking. My ego is always that big. It is one of the reasons I get so many women. It is also the reason I get into so much mess. Most times it is just me and my ego.

BTS:

Now that I had my Magnum on, I pulled her to me and started kissing over her body. I didn't know if she put on lotion or perfume, but she smelled like honey and she tasted like brown sugar and cinnamon. It sure tasted good and smelled even better. So I started at her right shoulder blade. I licked over to her left shoulder and around her neck twice. I licked down her back to the nape and then came back up. I went over to the left shoulder and down that whole side of her body and down to her feet. I then lay her down on the bed, flipped her over on her stomach, starting with the feet on up. I stayed right by her ass and licked her thighs from the back all inside of them.

She was moaning, "Yeah, yeah—that is what I call foreplay."

I continued to lick and lick. She started to shiver when I held her down and put my whole tongue in her ass. She was trying to get away. Then she stopped and just started shaking like she needed restraints. Her juices oozed down her legs.

"Goddamn it!" she hollered. "I have never..." She couldn't complete the sentence. So she started again. "I have never...."

I continued to lick and she was truly losing it. So I decided it was time to put in work. I turned her sideways, put her leg up on my shoulder and started stroking harder and harder. As I stroked deeper, I was penetrating so hard and so fast. As I was pumping, I started to think about every woman I had ever slept with. This was not a good feeling because it was like all of these bad thoughts were coming through. I was punishing her and she did not realize it.

"Yeah, yeah—that's it! You're the best," she said.

For real, I couldn't even feel anything. I just saw a body in front of me and my body moving.

Pause: I didn't know if I was dreaming or dead.

BTS:
I didn't have any feelings in my legs or anything else. I could see my dick. It was a big blob that kept moving in and out. I really didn't know what I was in. That actually scared me. What had I gotten myself into?

Pause: Let me flow –

Could this be
The worst thing that ever happened
The body part
That I love the most
Is somewhere else
That I am not familiar with
I am not sure if I will ever see
My friend again
Could this be
The end for me

BTS:
As I saw that blob again, I assumed it was my dick. Then it went in again and just disappeared. Now I was sobbing because I didn't have any feeling in it

anymore. But somewhere while I was going in and out, I felt a sharp pain in my groin area. I was just hoping it was just a pain.

Pause:

Maybe Gone
Not knowing this girl
Not knowing what she is capable of
Could she have done the unthinkable
Maybe gone
Still no feelings in the groin area
It better be there
But I am still in a daze even a maze
But could it be
I pray that it is still here
But could
It be gone

BTS:
I was coming out of the fog and I was in pain. What could that be that was hurting that much? Getting shot did not hurt that badly. It felt like I had been stabbed or cut with a sharp piece of glass. All of a sudden I was unconscious, but as I was feeling the pain, I was steadily praying. When I awoke, I found

myself in a puddle of blood. It was all over me and it was not all mine. Someone put my shorts on me. I was in constant pain. I was afraid to look to see if all of my equipment was still there. I got dressed and got the hell out of that hotel. I didn't know if that crazy broad would be back or what was going on. She did not rob me. So that must have been personal. When it's personal, they just came to hurt you. Basically they do like the Bible said—the devil does kill, steal, and destroy me. Why was I acting like I didn't have any enemies? For real, there were only a few people that actually liked me. I had dogged out so many people that they had started to come after me—men and women. Women because they had been in love and I never acknowledged any feelings toward them except having sex and giving me pleasure. The men were mad and after me because I didn't have a cut-card, meaning it didn't make a difference who I had sex with—from your sister to your niece to your momma. If she was of legal age and female, she might get it. I had tried to change and had been real good at changing. I had not done any mothers and daughters lately and I didn't plan to either. So I guess that was a confession that I had to myself. Really, I think I was going out of my head. All these thoughts started to get clearer. I wished they would stay fuzzy. For some strange reason, I could see these things clearly. It was not scaring me. It was just making me sad. How could one man—me—be so selfish? Where did I learn that nonsense? I wished I could blame that on someone else. But, for real, I just made myself. Instead of taking the good from folks and making myself a man from that which would have made me a gentleman, I took all the bad from most men and the sweet stuff that I knew would turn women inside out with their heart. I made myself a complete whore. I knew every aspect of manipulation. I knew how to turn on charm, even how to beg or have you beg. I had completely transformed myself into that person at one time in my life. I truly enjoyed that person I became. But lately I had started to despise that person—even hated that person—because I knew by being that person brought all the heartache and pain that I felt constantly. Now that I had myself halfway together, I knew I had to get out of that area NOW. I just started walking and walking. I ended up on my mother's street. But it was 4:00 a.m. I still had blood all over me. I knew I couldn't go see M. She would lose it, might die right there in my arms if she saw me like this. So I looked in my bag and got a pen and a small piece of paper. I wrote a note and put it in her mailbox.

Hey M,

I need to get away for a while. Please keep the business running and I will call you in a few weeks. I love you more today than yesterday, but not as much as I will love you tomorrow.

Love,
Your baby boy,
Courtney

BTS:

I walked up to Alabama Avenue to the bus stop and sat there until the bus came. It was a long, sobering ride. I got to 8th and H Streets and I had to transfer to another bus. That double bus pulled up and I got on. Within ten minutes, I was in front of Union Station. I got off the bus and walked into the building and everything was closed except the ticket counter. I fumbled through my bag and found my money, which was hidden in a little secret compartment. I got the money out and went to the counter. I looked at the signs for the next train to New York City. Then I asked the cashier for a one-way ticket to the big city.

She said, "You're talking about New York, right sir?"

"Yes Ma'am."

She could tell I was walking slowly and talking slurred and she asked if I was okay. I told her yes. She gave me the ticket. I gave her the money. Since I had been to Union Station numerous times before, I knew where everything was located. So I went to the men's room at the other end of the train station. This was where the homeless people were always hanging. By going to that bathroom, I knew I could just fit in and no one would notice the blood on me. I went into the stall and changed clothes. I washed off my face and hands. Then I brushed my teeth. Cleanliness was someplace I lived all my life. I couldn't stand being dirty and couldn't stand stinky people, especially women. Clean was sexy to me. So since I felt a tad bit better, I grabbed my bag, threw the old clothes in the trash, and left the bathroom. It was about twenty minutes later and I heard the announcement over the loud speaker that the 5:30 a.m. train, number 997 to New York, would be leaving from the bottom portal. I started to walk toward the portal. I felt steady pain. I still had not checked for my jewels.

Pause: Jewels — This is what a man would call his private parts. To break it down, it is his dick and balls.

BTS:

I was getting nervous because I didn't know why there was pain and I was terrified to check. I actually started wearing underwear. Even though I changed my pants, my underwear was still blood-soaked. Blood was running down my leg. I didn't know what to do. So I do the only thing I knew that worked. I started to pray.

> *Bleeding and hurting*
> *Is what is going on with me*
> *Not knowing and too*
> *Scared to look is*
> *Where I am*
> *Hurt and still hurting*
> *Please let this nightmare end*
> *Now I start my prayer*
> *It is me Lord*
> *Standing in the need of prayer*
> *Saying please release me, heal me*

Taboo V

Soothe me and make everything ok
In Jesus' name I pray
Amen-Amen-Amen

BTS:

In an instant, the blood stopped and I realized the power of prayer. I continued to walk toward the train. It seemed like that walk to the train was about three hours. I was still hurting. But it seemed like it was subsiding. I finally made it to the train and sat down at a window seat. I put my bag on the floor between my legs and snuggled up to the window and dosed off. While I was sleeping, I had the weirdest dreams. The first one was me having a conversation with my deceased grandmother. Mind you, I never met her on earth. She was dead before I was born. I had seen pictures of her. But I never had a live meeting. So that was very strange. She looked like my mother. We were in a park.

My grandmother said, "They call these the beer gardens." She told me my grandparents spent most of their days right there in that beer garden. "Come closer, baby." She sounded just like my mother.

I came closer.

As she talked, her voice had a calming effect.

"You are a good man with a whole lot of smarts. Baby, stop using your body as a weapon of pleasure." Then she said, "Won't you let somebody love you?" Then she was gone.

I was moving around trying to wake up. Then I saw a fine young lady that I had no idea who she was. I had a sister who died before I was born. So this was who I assumed it was. She was stillborn. So there were no pictures. As I got closer to her, she called out my full name, which very few people know.

"Come closer," she said.

I did as instructed.

She touched my hand and said, "Close your eyes and put your head toward the sky."

I did just that. As I touched her, I could see all of the things I did to women for the last ten years. As I turned toward the ground, it had dates, times and at the end it had how many women I had slept with. I looked at everything except how many women. Then there was another chart. It covered how many hearts I had broken. It was shattered in thousands of little pieces.

"What does all this mean?" I asked her.

"With you calling yourself Lil-Game to Mr. Roarke to owning the Zone, these are the hearts you broke. Most can never be repaired. Some are still working out the issues you put them through. Courtney, to put it bluntly, you were the wrong man. You can't do right until you decide you want to be the right man. The right man is a man that believes in someone bigger than him. It has to be a spiritual base, not just you thinking you're actually running something. Courtney, you don't run anything. So stop thinking you do." Then she disappeared.

Before I woke up, she returned and said, "Courtney, you will know when it is time because all you ever wanted to know about yourself and your family will be revealed." Then she disappeared again.

I finally woke up still amazed, terrified, and just down-right crazy. I didn't know what was going on. I wanted to leave that dream, nightmare, or disaster. I never wanted to be there again. I was starting to feel like this was my time to leave that earth. But I wanted to know if it was time, why was all that stuff being revealed? Was that another one of those signs that I really didn't want to acknowledge? I finally come out of the daze and made my way to the bathroom on the train. As I entered the bathroom, I doused my face with water.

Then I took a piss, washed my hands and left the bathroom. Pain was going through my legs and groin as I walked back to my seat. I decided not to go back to sleep for the next two hours. I just stared out the window. We finally made it to New York. I reached up and got my bags and slowly walked off the train to the cab stand. I decided to stay at another hotel instead of the Waldorf Astoria. It was in Manhattan. I just needed something different. I had the taxi drop me off there. I checked in and decided that I really needed a bath.

Pause: I have always told you a bath cured everything in my body, mind, and soul. And that time in my life, I needed all those things healed and fast.

BTS:
So there I was running bath water. I called downstairs because I didn't have bubble bath. So I asked for shampoo — no one needed to know I was about to take a bubble bath. When I called, I ask if I needed to come down. They said, "No." They said they would send someone up with it. In about five minutes, someone knocked on the door. I yelled, "Come in." I walked toward the door and I heard that voice.

"Mr. Edwards, I am here to drop off your shampoo. Hopefully it does not smell too feminine. It is the only kind we have."

As I got closer to the voice, I started to think I knew that voice. But I couldn't put a face to it. As I got closer, the voice said again, "Mr. Edwards, I am here if you need any other services." I finally got a glimpse of the person behind the voice. I looked at her. But I didn't know where I knew her from. I was wrapped up in a towel. Once she saw my face, she said, "Mr. Roarke, it's Sandy." My towel just dropped.

Recap: Who was Sandy? Sandy was the young lady that worked at the front desk of the Waldorf Astoria when Dre and I were last in New York. She was also the one that came to my door dressed as a maid that sexed me so good, I thought I was in love. But, she also left me the letter about how much she was in love with me.

PSA – Public Service Announcement
Men do it just as much as women. We fall in love over good sex. Not a good person – but – good sex. That was what happened with Sandy and myself. We fell in love over good sex. So the reason for the PSA was to know

the difference between good sex and a good person. Most times, they are not attached to the same person.

BTS:
So once I realized it was Sandy, I greeted her without picking up my towel. But my groin area was still in pain. I still had not looked down to check my equipment. She came over to grab me and looked down at my equipment and screamed, "Roarke! What happened to you?" I was breathless because I didn't want to look down. I was hurt, ashamed, and downright scared. I just went into a daze and said out loud:

What if what I have used to hurt or hook folks on
and love me was no longer
What if the body part I considered my prized
possession was dwindled down to worthless
What if I defined myself by that and that was all I
was
What if I can no longer perform the duties that I
think made me the man I thought I was
What if
What if
What if

BTS:

Now I was finally ready to address that situation. But that was just my mouth. My mouth had written a check that my body couldn't cash. Sandy came closer and got on her knees. She started peeling off skin and blood.

She looked up at me and said, "Roarke, I am here for you."

Tears were streaming down my face. I was not sure what was next. Then I saw tears streaming down her face. Now I was terrified.

I asked her hesitantly, "What's wrong?"

"Why? Why, Roarke, would you let someone do that to you?" Now we were both bawling.

Pause: I close my eyes and start to think of when my mother had to do surgery on my head after Catgirl had busted it. Now I am in New York and a woman I barely know is doing surgery on my most private part.

BTS:

I opened my eyes. Sandy now had tweezers, scissors, gauze, and alcohol. She was treating the wound with alcohol and I was continuously bleeding. I was feeling weak. But she was being so gentle, talking to me as she was finishing up her procedure. After she completed the surgery, she got off her knees and took a bow. I was dumbfounded now and actually a little mad.

"What the hell are you taking a bow for?"

"I just repaired you and you will live and your equipment will be just fine."

"So why am I still hurting?"

"I will get you some pain medicine, put you in the tub, and in a few weeks, you will be fine."

All I could do was thank her by saying, "You are too good for me. Why do you even want to help me after I just ran out on you a few weeks ago? I just sexed your brains out and tried to pull your insides out. Then you turn around and help me."

"Roarke, that was how I was raised. First, I should not have slept with you. But, I was going through a bad breakup with my boyfriend. The reason we were breaking up was because he said I was not adventurous enough."

"How could he say that? You came to my room in a maid's outfit. I thought that was adventurous."

"Yes, Roarke. I did that for you because you brought the freak out of me. He didn't."

Pause: Women — I have always said dress up for your man. This was a prime example. The man does not bring the freak out of you. It really was the outfit and your brain. All sexual functions start in the brain. The environment, clothing, and sometimes the other person enhance it. But it ultimately starts with the brain.

BTS:

She left the room and I lay in the bed. I was drifting off. In about thirty minutes, she returned. She gave me the medication as if she were a nurse or even my mother, which felt weird. Then she ran a warm bath and helped me get in. She washed me while I dozed off. That felt so good. It was like her touch was soothing. As much as I wanted to change, I still felt like the same Roarke—no good to anyone but myself. But that girl was just talking to me as she washed me. Her hands felt like they had baby oil in them. She slowly massaged me as she washed. After about twenty minutes, she helped me out of the tub. I was really in a daze now. She started to call me Courtney and whispered in my ear, "I promise to take care of you until you don't need me anymore."

Pause: That's a saying I used to say since I was 17 years old. I was the one to help put people's lives back together after a bad breakup or family drama. That was until my heart was broken and torn apart at 19. Then I became the person you know now. that has to be spiritual. I am coming full circle and it was starting to scare me.

BTS:

I was now in the bed sitting there totally amazed, scared and just didn't know what to do. So of course it was time to pray. But I was tired of praying and crying. I knew it was time for some real action on my part. But I was not sure what to do. So I shared these thoughts with Sandy.

"Sandy, I need to share something so deep and hurtful, I am not even sure I understand."

"Courtney, let me be your friend. I was your lover first which we both know was backwards. So let's start over. Remember I told you I was not going anywhere until you didn't need me anymore which I doubt was anytime soon. So please share your thoughts."

Pause: I really want to hide who I really am because for real, I am unsure of myself. Yes, even Mr. Roarke has difficulty with his own ego and self-consciousness.

BTS:

Sandy said, "Courtney, I am still waiting for your thoughts. Are you so confused—trying to figure out who you are, you couldn't even talk?"

I finally opened my mouth and said, "Yes, Sandy. I am actually afraid of who I have become. It was so ironic that I have become that person. They would say fate because this was the man I pictured my father as. All through childhood, I always wondered what he was thinking when he left and even more, what he was doing while he never had time to show my brother Shake and myself how to be good men. I am no longer mad at him because I think that was where I am right now. I am not agreeing with him leaving. I am just saying I understand where he was at the time. This was why I feel that women and men shouldn't have children until they are grown themselves."

PSA: Didn't have any unless you are willing to pay with your childhood. Or, only grown folks should have children.

BTS:

"Courtney, I understand where you are coming from. You only know what you have seen or heard—sometimes nothing more." I said, "You are so right."

"Courtney, that was why I am like that with people."

"Like what?"

"I am two people. My mother was what the old folks called fast. She slept with numerous people quickly. And that was what I did with you. But while my mother was being fast, my grandmother took care of me. We called her Nana and she cared for everybody from feeding them to fixing their wounds. She even put holes in your ears for earrings. She just cared for everybody. So I understand the personalities of you because I had to deal with them myself. But, Courtney, what you need to learn was when to just be yourself. Stop being who you patterned yourself after. I just learned how to be just me. I am no longer my mother or my Nana."

"Sandy I really understand what you are saying. But let me explain my position."

"Okay, Courtney. You have the floor."

"Now here it is. I have at least one hundred personalities in me. I have control of about ten of them. The other ninety are on their own. The ten that I control, eight of them are under the name,

Mr. Roarke. The other two are Courtney. At most times, I couldn't control the ones under Mr. Roarke and sometimes the other ninety get involved and whatever situation I am involved in just escalates into some unknown territory. That place scares even me because I never know what's going to happen. But I can say, most of the time it has been fun. A few times it has been dangerous. Reason being, Mr. Roarke was very protective of the other personalities. That means we all get in trouble."

Pause: One time, someone approached us from behind and Roarke thought they were coming to hurt us and he flipped. He choked the dude so hard, he blacked out. We all ran so fast, you would have thought we were Olympic sprinters. But all of my personalities have an appetite for the ladies. Courtney likes them educated and mild mannered. Mr. Roarke just likes pussy. He wants them just nasty. Roarke has no cut-cards. He will do your momma, sister, niece, and all your cousins. Lately Roarke has been doing educated women who are nastier. They are college educated. But they are still freaks. They were too busy getting ahead. They never had a chance to get their freak on.

BTS:

"So do you prefer I call you Roarke or Courtney? It seems that most of the times, you are actually Roarke. So when are you Courtney?"

"For real Sandy, I didn't know."

"Let me finish getting you well. Then we can explore all of your personalities and other folks in my head that I have not shared."

My Head
Why was it hurting
Which personality was trying to get out
I am having hot and cold spells
Now I am dizzy
The intense pressure
Is sickening
The reactions and the inability
To change that feeling
Makes me want to hide
Then after the constant hurt
A new personality appears
Hi I am Delvan
I rule the world
My head

BTS:

Now Sandy was looking totally amazed. "Roarke... Courtney, I have to say that and please didn't take it the wrong way."

"Say it. I can take it."

"You crazy and you know it. But the biggest difference in you and most others was that you are totally functional. Most folks would not even realize how many people are inside of you. Also, they would not imagine how brilliant you are. I know you run a successful business and that you also work full-time, and have a very active social life along with some incredible late night skills."

"Thanks Sandy for the kind words. It was nice when people actually understand me. The only person that understood me was my mother and she was the only person that did not judge me which I truly miss and love about her. I would be lost if she leaves that earth — just devastated. She was my world. I actually worship her. She was the apple of my eye."

My mother
My best friend
Roses and sugar
Everything I consider sacred
Really the only person
I ever loved
The only person that
Actually loved me
Only person greater is
GOD

BTS:

"Wow, Courtney, that poem was brilliant. You amaze me. I did not know you were a poet."

"Sandy, I amaze myself. All of the things that I do are effortless. Most folks have all that training to do the things that I do. But it all comes naturally for me, including the business. There are so many personalities within me and they all come together to create all the things I do. So sometimes, they are really good and other times, they are deadly."

She said, "Roarke, let's see if we can have a relationship."

Two people as one
She wants a relationship
I just want to survive that trip
She says we can work it out
I just want to live to be forty
She says I have been waiting
On you all my life
I said why me and why now
She says my knight in shining armor
I say never been a knight
Don't want to start now
She said well Damn
Why are you here
My response, if I knew
I would not be here any longer
Then there was a perplexed look on her face
My response was didn't ask a question that
You really didn't want an answer to

BTS:

So as we complete, which was not a pleasant event, we just stared into space. It was like we were looking into the air as if all our dreams, emotions, fears, and tears would just appear or disappear. Now, since we had been staring for what seems like an eternity, I asked her now that we were here in New York City and I planned to stay for a while, what would we do? Would we become a couple, best friends, lovers, or has she even thought that far? She sat there dumbfounded, not knowing what move to make or even if she should speak.

Pause: So it's up to me to decide our destiny. God knows I am tired of deciding other folk's destiny.

BTS:

I tell her I wanted to remain friends first and work toward a relationship. She still had not moved or opened her mouth. So there I sat again with another woman that does not want to follow her own path in life.

Pause:

Life's Path
We all want to know
We have been on
This journey
Our whole life
Life's path
As a child
We look toward
Our parents
To direct us then
School somewhere
Along the line
We should at least
Have some direction
But sadly most times
We didn't even know ourselves

BTS:
It was starting to get later in the day and I was feeling so tired. So Sandy and I agreed to just end our day together.

The End

Dearest Readers:

I would first like to thank you for your continued support of the Taboo Series — from buying books, T-shirts and showing up in mass numbers for Taboo Raw and Uncut sessions in person. My words can't express my deepest feelings of gratitude, so I will sum them up with: *Thanks for being incredibly awesome!*

ACKNOWLEDGMENTS

First I need to thank God; without him there would be no me.

My "thank yous" are few, with a more realistic approach of who really helped me.

My unconditional lover...

Judy Samantha Harrison: sometimes you were the blood that flowed through my veins, but God loved you more. May you keep making people smile as you brighten up heaven. My days and spirit are stress-free because of YOU. I celebrate twenty-two awesome years with you and two terrific kids. May the heavens forever shine now that you have arrived.

Rojena and Robert, the other angels watching over me, love you always.

Michelle Coles-Johnson, Jessica Tilles, Troy Rawlings, Kayla Harrison, Rodney Harrison, Jr., Austin and Danielle Henderson, Tonya and Tania Frederick, Marvin Wray, Pat Goree, Ruth, Kristin, Marsha ,Maurice, Pete, Ryan, Brandon, Melvin, Robyn, Rocky, Ronda Brian, Christopher, Michael, and Hollywood and Ryze radio family.

Timing and Effort

Each of you have lent yourselves through time and money, and most of all your hearts and I am grateful to call them FAMILY!

www.ingramcontent.com/pod-product-compliance
Lightning Source LLC
Chambersburg PA
CBHW020625250626
47154CB00004B/1678